Tumbling
HEAD OVER
Heels

KACIE WEST

Jess

Enjoy this fake
fiancée romance

X Kacie West

Tumbling
HEAD OVER
Heels

JENNI BARA AND AJ RANNEY WRITING AS
KACIE WEST

Tumbling Head Over Heels

Copyright @ 2023 Kacie West

All rights reserved.

The book is a work of fiction. The characters and events in this book are fictitious. Any similarity to real persons, living or dead, is purely coincidental and not intended by the author.

Developmental Edit by Katie Bockino

Line, Copy, Proofreading by Beth Lawton at VB Edits

Interior formatting by H.C. PA & Formatting Services

ISBN: 979-8-9859485-6-1 (ebook)

ISBN: 979-8-9859485-7-8 (paperback)

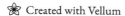 Created with Vellum

To every Kelly out there stumbling through life trying to find herself.

"Don't screw this up." His boss's threat echoed in Jack's ear as the automatic glass doors opened in front of him. The cool, damp air smacked against his cheeks as he hurried through the throngs of people outside the Asheville airport.

Getting out of the congested terminal was worth weathering a little rain. He hated flying commercial. Small seats, cramped legs, loud children, and endless lines all made his skin crawl. But a last-minute change of plans meant the company jet was in New York with his father and unavailable to get Jack from LA to Ashville.

"We need this account, and the Hills aren't happy that lovable Larry isn't coming to woo them."

He gripped the phone tighter. If his colleague's wife hadn't gone into labor early, he never would have been given another opportunity to prove himself. Even if the Nickles Group was *Jack's* father's company, Larry was the favorite.

Ahead of him, another line had formed at the curb. He'd have to fight through the crowd to find his waiting Uber. "I've got this. Trust me."

Dan snorted into the phone. After how wrong the last *situ-*

ation had gone, he couldn't blame his boss for his doubts. But that issue had been personal. This was business.

He wasn't a family man like Larry, but he had a golden tongue. Need a man to sell stripes to a tiger? He was the guy. The guy who'd never heard the word no. Even off the cuff, he could toss around an endless number of ideas. The hours he'd had to plan ways to market the vitamin water as a healthy alternative to sugary sports drinks made locking in a long-term deal with the Hills a cake walk.

He might've gotten an immediate position with his dad's firm because of his last name, but he would prove that he deserved more than the low-level account manager position he was stuck in.

"Watch it," Jack snapped as a punk-ass kid barreled toward him, narrowly missing a head-on collision. Interactions like this were exactly why he hated airports. The teenager flipped him off, and with a frown, Jack worked his way along the busy sidewalk, trying to ignore the drizzle.

His boss was still yammering in his ear, but Jack pulled the phone away and scanned the screen to verify the Uber information as he stepped to the curb. He jumped back as a car rolled by, sending water crashing over the sidewalk. Damn, he didn't have time for this.

If he hadn't used every minute of the last twelve hours to work on pitch ideas, he would've had a car service booked.

He'd found Uber to be as unreliable as the weather. Jack much preferred to have Stan, his driver, on standby, waiting to load his bag and with a preplanned traffic-free route in his GPS. Stan always used an Escalade so Jack's legs didn't cramp on the drive home. But he was more than two thousand miles from home, so he'd have to make do with the dipshit Uber driver assigned to him. Spotting the small silver sedan listed on the app, he headed that way. The driver had the visor down and was applying lipstick, ignoring him and the airport chaos. Fucking great. He couldn't be late for this meeting, so Miss Hot Lips needed to snap to attention. This was his last chance to prove he was more than just the CEO's son.

Not to mention, he could use the opportunity to prove to his dad that he wasn't a complete fuck-up. His stomach turned at the memory of his father's face. Lately, all he'd seen when his dad looked at him was disappointment. It was time to change that.

When he yanked open the door, the woman fumbled her lipstick, dropping it in her lap in the process. Her blue eyes widened in shock before she shook her head and sent him a tight smile. He pointed to the phone at his ear, thankful she'd gotten the message and remained silent as he took his overcoat off and tossed it on the seat.

"I won't relax until you can assure me you won't be sleeping with the client's wife or daughter or niece or, fucking hell, *granddaughter*," Dan all but growled.

Jack winced as he unbuttoned his suit jacket and slid into the back seat. With one look at the dingy floorboard, he set his garment bag beside him. Glancing at the fabric seat, he couldn't help but turn his nose up in disgust. His leather bag was probably worth more than the car. If his suit got stained, he'd be pissed. Another reason he should have ordered a car service.

"Do you hear me? I expect you to be the most well-mannered, upstanding citizen they've ever met," Dan groused, his elevated voice pulling Jack back to the moment. "I'm talking choir boy, here."

"Yeah, got it." Jack ground his teeth. He was sick of defending the same action over and over. It was a one-time thing, and the woman never mentioned being married when *she* came on to him. How was he supposed to know she was his newest client's wife?

"I *mean* it. Even your old man won't save your ass this time."

"Got it. I'm in the Uber now." He peered over the front seat at the driver. The young brunette was focused on the road in front of her. "I'm heading straight to the meeting at the resort, and then I'll check into my room after that."

"You better." His boss ended the call without another word.

Jack pulled out his laptop, determined to prove he wasn't the fuck-up his father believed him to be. This trip would go so smoothly that his father, his boss—everyone—would be forced to eat their words about him. He was *not* an utter screw-up.

GOOD THING she hadn't stopped for gas. There was no doubt Kelly would have been late to pick up her fare if she had. And the suit in the back seat didn't seem like the type who put up with bullshit. She stole another glance at the man in the review mirror. Tension rolled off him in waves. The cuff of his navy suit slipped up his wrist, showing off an expensive watch, as he raked his long fingers through his dirty-blond hair. His hand hit the ceiling above him, and he tipped his head up and glared, his vibrant green eyes blazing. As tall as the suit dude was, he should be a pro at squishing into cars, but he frowned at the gray upholstery like it was out to get him.

Blowing out a breath, she turned her attention back to the road, immediately hitting the brakes and skidding a bit on the wet asphalt. The rain was starting to come down hard now.

Suit dude muttered an expletive as they both jerked forward at the sudden slow down, and something jammed into the back of her seat, knocking her again.

"Sorry." She cringed. "Is your laptop okay?"

"Just watch the road." He clenched his smooth jaw and glared at her through the mirror.

Great. Suit dude had either never learned manners, or he was just an asshole. She twisted the knob that controlled the wiper speed, adjusting the pace from swift to the flapping of a hummingbird's wings. The *thwat* of the rubber echoed in the silent car as she squinted into the rain.

Airport runs were the worst. Nine times out of ten, her fares were cranky after long days of travel. She much preferred picking up people who were on their way to a night out or coming home after. They were usually chatty and fun. Possibly the only good thing about this Uber gig was chatting with the random people she picked up in her free time, but the second job was necessary if she wanted to get herself out of the hole she'd created.

"I'm Kelly," she prompted hopefully, but he didn't respond. The traffic crept along, but once they got past the downtown area, the road would open up. "Is the traffic going to make you late?"

"It better not." He scoffed.

The man didn't have an obvious accent, but the suit, the stress, and the bad attitude had her betting he was from New York. Too bad the crappy personality came in such a good-looking package. He had a chiseled jaw, a straight nose, and gorgeous eyes, but his general jerkiness dimmed any attraction. She waited for him to add to the conversation, but he kept his eyes on his laptop and ignored her.

Awesome. It would be a long hour's drive at this rate. Focusing on the road again, she tried to come up with something to entertain herself. She started the alphabet game, finding words that started with each letter on the signs she passed. When she was searching for *K*, she was startled by the deep timbre of his voice. She opened her mouth, super ready to chat with the guy, but quickly realized he was on the phone again. He rattled off numbers before diving into a monologue using words like *lucrative*, *abdicate*, and *pivotal*.

Who the heck talked like that? Ugh. Big SAT words were for pompous douches who were trying to convince people they were smarter than they actually were. No one used those words in everyday life. Ashley, her boss at the catering company—Kelly's day job—would look at her like she lost her damn mind if she used *abdicate* in a sentence.

She tapped the brake as she exited the freeway, cursing the damn heels. Flats were better for driving, but she hadn't planned to pick up fares today. Her boss had sent her to Ashville for an appointment with the local bakery, but when the fare popped up, she couldn't resist earning a little extra money to recoup what she'd spent on gas.

Half Moon Lake, the small-town where Kelly lived, was almost an hour from the city, and her wallet didn't have the extra cash needed for the expense of today's trip to the bakery. She'd cringed at the idea of admitting that to Ashley, so she'd sucked it up and accepted that she'd have to charge the price of gas to her almost maxed-out credit card.

Christmas had messed up her budget, and she'd been trying to get back on track since. Her shoulders slumped at the reminder. She had to figure her shit out. Quitting nursing school and, in turn, getting cut off by her parents, had turned her life into a dumpster fire. Career wasn't currently her word. But catering and driving for Uber weren't going to work out permanently—that much had become clear.

Lights in the distance flashed, causing Kelly to squint. It was the first car she'd seen since they'd gotten off the highway, and her eyes just didn't adjust. She kept her focus on the road in front of her, shielding herself with her hand so the bright headlights of the oncoming car didn't blind her.

The fuel estimator on her dash had dropped from twenty or so miles to *low fuel* at some point in the last twenty minutes—she wasn't exactly sure when. But the GPS said that they only had sixteen miles to go. She'd gone farther on low fuel before.

The glowing white and red sign ahead caught her attention, but it was obvious that suit dude wasn't the type who'd appreciate a pit stop.

"Could you turn on the heat, or is it broken?" Boy, did he have a tone.

Typically, Kelly would, especially since she hadn't brought a sweater with her. But she couldn't remember whether it was the heat or the air that used gas. Hesitantly she clicked the heat back on, letting the warm air hit her face. She couldn't afford another bad Uber review.

"Heading to an important meeting?" she asked now that he was once again off the phone.

"I prefer a silent ride." He didn't even look her way, just kept his eyes on the screen in front of him.

"It's probably better that way. I don't have a big enough vocabulary to talk to you," she huffed.

"What?" he asked.

She met his gaze in the mirror. Even if he was a total tool bag, his green eyes were gorgeous. That was undeniable.

"I'm not sure I even know what epochal means."

He huffed a breath and went back to focusing on his laptop.

Five miles into the climb to the resort tucked into the North Carolina mountains, her car sputtered, and it almost seemed like the engine coughed, making the weirdest noise she ever heard.

What the heck?

After one more almost snort, the engine died. The car rolled slowly as Kelly steered to the shoulder. When she'd pulled the car off the road as far as she could, she hit the brake so they wouldn't roll down the steep incline of the hill. Why on earth would the car stop? Her eyes widened.

Was this what it sounded like when it ran out of gas?

3

"WHY DID YOU STOP?" Jack snapped, wincing at his biting tone. This chick might be annoying, but he wasn't purposely trying to be rude as fuck. Between being crammed into the tin can of an airplane seat for six hours, getting whacked in the knee by the beverage cart twice, the dressing down he'd gotten from his boss, *and* the bumper-to-bumper highway traffic, Jack was holding on to his patience by a thread.

His meeting with the owners of Hill Water started in less than an hour, and this chick had randomly pulled over on a deserted winding road.

"Uh..." Kelly's brows pulled together, and she tilted her head to the side. "I think"—she swallowed—"maybe, um, we ran out of gas."

How the fuck was that a question? Cars, even shitty-ass ones like this, had gauges and idiot lights so drivers could avoid this exact scenario. Running out was never a surprise.

"Was that a possibility?" What kind of Uber driver ran out of *gas*?

"Well." She studied the road ahead of them, no longer meeting his eyes in the mirror. "I mean, at the airport, it was like forty-three miles to empty, and the resort was only thirty-seven miles away, so it's kinda weird."

"But we sat in traffic for a half hour." How the hell did she not realize that would use more gas?

Kelly chuckled. "Plus we used the heat."

"You've got to be shitting me." His head was going to explode, and she was fucking laughing. He ran his hand through his hair, whacking the headliner again. He glared up, fisting his hand, trying his best to not punch through the fabric and metal.

His heart sped up as unease shifted down his spine. He might miss the most important meeting of his life because he was stuck on the side of the road in backwoods country. He blew a hard breath into his fist. Panicking wouldn't help. Pulling out his phone, he silently willed a second bar to appear on the cellular service readout as the Uber app loaded.

"Over an hour for another car." He held back a shout of frustration. He shouldn't be surprised. They were in the middle of fucking nowhere. *Do not panic.* He would have to Zoom into the meeting and explain the situation to the Hill family. Surely, they knew that getting around in Bumblefuck mountain country wasn't easy.

"I have roadside assistance," the chick piped up, turning in her seat. "I'll get them out here as soon as possible. So sorry about this. I, uh, don't know what happened."

"Let me help you understand," he snapped. "The car makes this *ding*, and a light flashes, telling you 'hey, idiot, you're almost out of gas. Stop and get some.' Most people do exactly that, and since you didn't, we ran out."

Instead of looking remorseful, Kelly raised a brow at him and smirked. "No big words for me this time?"

This chick was amazingly frustrating. "We passed a motel half a mile back. I'll walk there and get a room. Best of luck, Kelly."

He threw open his door and winced. A gust of wind sent the cascading rain into the car, soaking his pant leg. It was dark as sin up here on the mountain, pouring, and cold. He glanced at the pretty woman in the seat in front of him. Her teeth were pressed nervously into her lip as she scanned the empty road.

She'd be fine. Right? He took in the dark woods surrounding them. They weren't even on a shoulder. She'd just pulled halfway off the winding road. One car coming a bit too fast around the curve, and this car would get hit. His conscience, that he wanted so badly to ignore, screamed at him. He checked his phone and groaned. He couldn't leave this chick alone in Bumblefuck to get hit. Clearly life skills weren't Miss *I don't know how I ran out of gas*'s strong suit.

Gritting his teeth, he bit out. "This isn't safe. You'll get hit by a car or be murdered by a backwoods psycho if I leave you here. You'll have to come with me."

"What?" she asked, spinning around to look at him over the seat.

"As much as I'd love to leave you out here to fend for yourself, I'm not that much of an asshole. And I don't have time to argue. So get out of the car. We're walking to the motel." He shot her the best *don't test me* look he could muster until, finally, she gave him a nod.

Thank fuck.

Her bare arm caught his attention when she cracked her door and the dim dome light came on. What the hell was this chick wearing? Short sleeves? She climbed out, leaving the silver door open and wrapping her arms around herself. Long chestnut waves that were immediately soaked fell past her shoulders and ample breasts. The flimsy white shirt quickly became a second skin as the rain pelted every inch of her body. She was all gorgeous curves and smooth skin. Beautiful women were his kryptonite. Or maybe his favorite addiction.

He blinked and frowned hard before he let that train of thought leave the station.

He could not go there. Not this time. *No women.*

"Get back in the damn car," he growled.

He didn't care if she was the most beautiful creature God had ever created, she was not distracting him from the prize.

She blinked at him blankly. "Why?"

"You're getting soaked." He gave her a once-over, forcing himself to focus on the ridiculousness of her attire. Short sleeves and heels in this weather? He was right. Clearly, she was life-skill deficient.

"Grab your coat." He sighed when she climbed back into the driver's seat.

She opened her mouth but didn't speak. Then she spun and frowned at him. "I don't know your name."

"Jack," he said. "Coat. Put it on." He waved a hand at her bare arms.

"Uh, Jack." She scrunched up her nose. "I'm not a big coat person."

"*What?*" The fuck does that mean?

"They're bulky, and it's hard to find cute ones that work with outfits."

Were his eyes bugging out of his face? It sure as shit felt like it. "It's forty degrees." He crossed his arms over his chest. "It's cold." They weren't in freaking LA, where coats were optional accessories. In these conditions, they were necessary.

She rolled her eyes. "Thanks, Captain Obvious." But she shivered. "I wasn't expecting to run out of gas and need to walk somewhere. Duh."

How could anyone be this ridiculous? Jack didn't have time to debate common sense with someone so clearly lacking in it, so he passed his wool overcoat over the seat to her.

Rather than accept the gesture, she looked at the coat warily.

"I'm sorry it won't match your outfit." He couldn't hold back the sarcasm.

But after watching him for another long moment, she put the damn thing on. With his hands on the headrests, he heaved himself up, scanning the floorboard of the front seat for her umbrella. He didn't see one up there. Just her ridiculous shoes. Heels in the rain.

"Where's the umbrella?" Jack searched the back. Nothing. A slight itch of worry tickled his brain. Half a mile in the pouring rain would suck.

He settled back in the seat.

"Umbrella?" With her head cocked to the side and an adorable crease between her brow, she stared at him blankly.

"You know, the thing you hold over your head in the rain?"

"I know what it is." She rolled her big blue eyes. "I just can't imagine why you think I'd have one."

His eye felt funny. Was it twitching? He let out a long exhale, hoping to force some of his building frustration out with it. How had this woman made it this far in life with such a lack of common sense? There had to be an umbrella somewhere in this car. Someone had to help this woman out with things like umbrellas. He turned, glancing over the seat to the small area behind him. There sat a long red umbrella. His shoulders sagged in relief as he pulled it over the seat. Once he'd opened the back door again, he stuck the umbrella out into the rain, then hauled himself out into the night. Kelly stepped quickly next to him, wrapped up in the oversized wool coat.

"Let's get moving. I need to make it there before my meeting. Can you walk quickly in those?" He nodded at her feet.

"Probably." Her forehead creased in the cutest way, like she was contemplating his question.

Jack shook his head and grabbed his briefcase before turning and starting down the street. Once they got to the hotel, he'd have to get rid of this girl. Hopefully, she could call someone local to get her. Maybe a boyfriend.

Oddly, he frowned at that idea. Why did the thought bother him so much? Although she probably made the poor man insane, he could take her off Jack's hands. Because he could *not* get distracted. His career was on the line and he had to stay focused. So the gorgeous brunette needed to go. Quickly.

4

Did he have to walk so fast? When she said she could walk in her heels, she hadn't meant like a *run* walk. Freaking wedges. She should keep a pair of flats in her car so she'd have them when plans changed. *Note to self: put shoes in car.* She probably wouldn't remember that tip five minutes from now, but whatever.

"What's this meeting for?" Kelly finally broke the silence as they hurried along the side of the road.

"Vitamin water. I need to convince them that the Nickles Group is the best choice if they want to move on to the next level."

Huh. Water. She chuckled.

"Jack and Jill went up the hill to fetch a pail of water," she sang.

"What?" Jack asked, spinning toward her and cocking a brow, his eye developing a weird tic. It was almost like the one her dad got. Her brother-in-law Tim did it too sometimes.

Hmm. Weird. Was it a common thing in men?

"What are you talking about?" Jack repeated, jarring her back to their conversation.

"Oh." She shrugged, forcing herself to remember what she'd said. "You know. Like the nursery rhyme about Jack and Jill?"

"Isn't your name Kelly?"

"Uh, yes." Did he have memory issues?

He opened his mouth, but slammed it shut immediately. Though his eye definitely twitched again as he spun away from her and continued down the road, all while mumbling to himself. She couldn't make out what he was saying.

"Are you talking to me?" she finally asked.

He cleared his throat. "I'm going to get a room at the motel so I can jump into my meeting. Is there someone you can call to help you with your car?"

Uck. Her car. She'd call AAA and—oh no.

She couldn't call AAA. That was her dad's account. Crap. She tucked her hair behind her ear. Being self-sufficient was what she'd wanted. She needed to make her own life choices. Prove she was perfectly capable of adulting. But adulting, it turned out, was complicated. She was learning. On a curve. Clearly today's was a steep one.

"Kelly?" he prompted.

Huh? Oh right. Her car.

"Yeah, I'll call someone."

But who? Her parents would say *I told you so*. She could call one of her brothers-in-law, though. She was only twenty minutes from Half Moon Lake. Tim could bring her gas. No biggie. Her mom and dad wouldn't have to know that she still hadn't figured out her crap.

Really, she wasn't doing too bad. She'd only been on her own for six months.

She pulled the huge coat tighter in hopes of blocking the cool, wet air. It smelled like a mix of cedar and rain. As she pressed her nose to the fabric and pulled in another breath, her foot slipped, and she skidded, teetering on her cursed heels.

Automatically, she threw an arm out and grabbed hold of Jack to steady herself.

Through his coat, she could feel the hard planes of his body as his breath danced against her cheek and his strong jaw brushed against her temple. She swallowed hard at the first inkling that her stomach may flip, keeping the response at bay.

"I thought you said you could walk in those." He narrowed his green eyes and pulled her in tighter for a split second before he stepped back and cleared his throat.

"Yeah. I do it all the time, but it's slippery."

His eye twitched again. "That's why you shouldn't wear shoes like that during rainstorms."

"I wasn't planning on hiking down a mountain today."

"Has anyone ever told you your planning leaves a lot to be desired?" He shook his head.

Yeah, she'd heard it from just about everyone she knew. She huffed out a breath. "Has anyone ever told you you're a bit of an asshole?"

"If I was an asshole, you'd be sitting alone in the car." He smirked and headed toward the entrance of the roadside motel. He was still holding the umbrella, so she was forced to keep up.

She hadn't taken more than three steps before the roar of an engine sounded behind her. As if the moment had been scripted, she peered over her shoulder just in time to watch a car splash through an icy puddle, the sludge spraying her from head to toe down one side.

Jack's suppressed chuckle had her shooting a glare his way. Of course Mr. Sparkle Pants was left untouched. But the joke was on him.

"Glad you think this is funny. Especially since I'm wearing your jacket."

His smile faded and his lips turned down, that eye twitch returning in full force before he continued ahead of her.

She shook as much of the sludge from the coat as she could before giving her hair a good shake too.

"Hurry up," Jack snapped, holding the glass door open. Once they were in the small lobby of the motel, he pulled a credit card from his wallet and threw it down on the counter.

"I need a room. Quickly."

"Please," she added.

The jerk's jaw locked, but he fixed his scowl on the counter in front of him.

"This is the asshole stuff I'm talking about."

"*Please*," he said through gritted teeth.

The attendant swiveled his head back and forth between Jack and Kelly before saying, "We don't rent by the hour anymore."

The grump beside her crossed his arms over his chest with a smirk. "Doesn't matter. I'll pay for the night. Just need it quick."

"By the hour?" That was a thing? Why? Did they get a lot of people running out of gas on this road?

Jack glared at her, his emerald irises burning with irritation. "It's fine. Neither of us should care what he thinks."

She tucked her hair behind her ear, shuddering at the gritty dampness of it. Uck. She needed a shower. She couldn't even wash and dry her hair in an hour.

"I don't get it. Why would anyone rent a room for only an hour?"

His brows rose high on his forehead. "You're kidding, right?"

She shook her head.

"He thinks you're a hooker."

Her eyes snapped up to the man behind the desk.

"He *what*?" she squeaked.

The attendant shrugged and held out the keycard.

"Why am I the hooker and not him?" Kelly asked the man behind the counter.

Jack closed his eyes and let out a huff. When he opened them again, his eye did that twitching thing once more.

"Miss," the man began. "You're beautiful. You don't need to pay men to sleep with you. I'd even do it for free."

Jack snorted.

"Aww, thank you." Kelly couldn't help but return the man's smile. "I'll be a hooker then."

Jack grabbed her arm. "No, you will *not*." His voice was tight even as he moved them away from the counter. "How have you survived this long?"

"Survived? What do you mean?" she asked, tugging against his grasp as he dragged her outside.

"Telling a random man you'll be a hooker is the definition of epochal stupidity."

She glared at his use of SAT words, anger tightening her gut. "I still don't know what that means."

"Unparalleled," he spit out, his eye twitching a little faster than it had earlier.

Head tilted, she asked, "You mean like very stupid?"

"*Yes*."

"Why don't you just say that?" She rolled her eyes. "Then you wouldn't sound like you have a stick up your butt."

"How old are you?" he demanded. His attention flicked down to the room key before he glanced to the balcony of labeled doors.

"Twenty-three." She scanned the doors that faced where they stood. "Top floor, second from the end."

"What?" he snapped.

"Room one fourteen is the second door from the end."

"Let's go." He turned and stormed toward the stairs.

Yeah, that wasn't the smartest idea—epochal stupid or

whatever. The whole renting a room thing, then laughing about being a hooker. Now following this guy up?

He peered over his shoulder at her before freezing and spinning around. "Why aren't you moving? You're getting soaked."

"You know I'm not actually a hooker, right?"

"Fuck's sake." He shut his eyes and took a deep breath. "I'm not the one who said you were a hooker. I don't have time for this." The knuckles of the hand he held the umbrella pole with were turning white. "I have to get set up for a meeting. I've been prepping for it for the last twelve hours, and it's going to make or break my career. Come into the damn room and sit quietly so I don't have to worry that you'll end up murdered or hit by an oncoming car," he waved a hand at her, "or become a hooker."

Kelly scoffed. "You're like supes paranoid."

"Supes?" His gaze snapped to hers.

"It's how normal people say *very*." She shrugged.

Everything from his tense shoulders to his clenched fists, even the hard lines his thin lips formed, screamed *stressed.* "Please, just sit in my room and wait for whoever the hell you're calling. It's cold, and I'll eventually need my jacket back."

She tried to cross her arms, but the coat got in the way. She held her hands up and shook them until the sleeves slid halfway down her forearms. Then she tried again, but the meaning of the gesture was lost because the coat was entirely too big.

"Fine," she agreed and trudged up the stairs behind him.

Once they were in the room, she couldn't help but laugh at the look on Jack's face. For all his talk about renting rooms by the hour, he obviously had never been in a cheap motel.

"Is something wrong?" She bit into her cheek to hold back a smile.

"This is disgusting. People actually sleep here?" His green eyes were wide and horrified.

But the room wasn't all that bad. It kinda looked like the

place she and her friends had stayed for spring break during her sophomore year in college. Truthfully, this might have been better than the motel in Daytona.

"If they rented these rooms by the hour at some point, they probably were mostly used for sex." She almost regretted her words when he turned and his heated gaze raked over her. She'd taken his coat off, and his attention lingered on her chest. A current snapped through her as he tipped his chin up and made eye contact.

"We are not having sex." But he didn't sound convinced.

She shivered. The man might be annoyed AF with her, but she knew what turned on looked like.

"Duh." Her laugh died in her throat before it even really started. Damn.

He pointed to the bed. "Sit and be quiet. Don't move until I'm done with this meeting."

5

THIS WAS GOING SURPRISINGLY WELL, given the clusterfuck the day had become. Repositioning himself on the dilapidated chair, he accidentally kicked the leg of the piece of crap table and swallowed a curse as his laptop shook. The rectangle he appeared in on the screen jolted, making it look like he'd just experienced an earthquake. He was used to hotel suites with desks and office chairs, not tables that folded up at the slightest provocation.

Surprisingly, Kelly didn't appear to be offended by the room. He'd never met a woman who wouldn't have run away screaming the second she opened the door to this filthy hellhole. But Kelly? She had taken it all in stride. Once she'd made herself comfortable on the edge of the mattress, she'd made a call to some guy and explained her car situation. Then she'd sat quietly and played on her phone. The woman was a confusing mix of insanely frustrating and crazy easy-going.

"Right, Jack?" his boss asked.

Jack shook his head to clear it, spitting out a few numbers and some ideas about how to drive the brand.

Since his boss in California had to join the meeting as well,

Zoom access was already set up for those who couldn't make it down for the conference this week. The Hills were understanding about his need to join online instead of in person. Apparently, getting reliable ride shares around this area *was* tough. It explained how Tweedle Dee had become an Uber driver.

Dan, on the other hand, was a different story. He had been pissed when Jack called to fill him in. On top of that, he had a hard time believing Jack's ludicrous play-by-play of the day's events. Because it was fucking ludicrous. This chick was from la-la land.

He didn't mention that his young, gorgeous Uber driver was currently holed up in the tiny-ass hotel room with him. That seemed like a bad idea. Especially considering his history.

He hadn't kept Kelly around because she was hot. That was more of an annoying *but also*. Holy hell, when she'd talked about sex while standing in front of the dingy bed, her damp shirt still stuck to her curves, Jack's brain clocked how fast he could get her naked. *Twenty-three seconds.* And he'd bet on that. He was lightning with a bra clasp. But he was thirty-four, and sex with a woman more than ten years younger than him would only prove his dad right—that he was a fuck-up.

In his entire life, Jack had never met a more incapable person. And his conscience wouldn't let him leave her until she was safely handed off to whoever the hell she'd called to rescue her. But could this guy even be trusted? If Jack's experience with her was any indication, the answer was hell no.

"Jack's been working hard on this, and his ideas are spot on." Dan pulled him back to the meeting.

"I have a few suggestions about the demographic we should cater marketing to—"

"Who's that?" The voice of one of the Hill siblings echoed around the room.

The man narrowed his eyes, craning his neck, and his sister

mimicked the move, like they were looking behind Jack. There was only one other person in the room, so the image reflecting on his computer screen could only be Kelly, but Jack swore he'd told her to sit the fuck down. His face felt funny, like he'd developed a tic around his eye in the last hour. How hard was it to follow directions?

Jack glanced over his shoulder, shooting figurative daggers at her.

Kelly shrugged and silently mouthed, "Sorry. Had to pee."

Didn't that sound exactly like the crazy, frustrating woman he'd been dealing with for the last few hours? When the bathroom door clicked shut, he slumped his shoulders. Turning back to the screen, he was met with Dan's scowl. Shit. He'd better come up with a damn good reason for being in a shady motel room with a random woman. And in truth, he had one—he was a decent man, and he refused to leave a woman who was a few French fries short of a Happy Meal alone on a dark road —but he'd pushed his limits with Dan already. The man wouldn't believe a word of his explanation. He knew that as well as he knew his name. Likewise, the Hill siblings had probably heard rumors of Jack's philandering ways, which wouldn't do him any favors on his mission to convince them that he was their guy.

He had to be quick on his feet.

"That's Kelly"—he swallowed hard, his vocal cords fighting against the next words—"my fiancée."

Fuck. Though it was complete and utter bullshit, the phrase caught in his throat. He could have gone with girlfriend or sister. Hell, he should have told them she was the Uber driver who'd run out of gas. But no, fiancée was what his brain required him to utter.

When the haze of panic cleared, all he could see were beaming smiles. Every one of them looked thrilled. Except his boss, who silently telegraphed *you're full of shit* and—maybe —*you better pull this off*.

"We didn't realize you were bringing someone with you," the youngest of the Hills, a woman in her fifties, said. "I'm excited to meet her. You can learn a lot about a man by getting to know the woman who stands beside him."

Fuckity fuck, fuck.

He could get out of this. *Lie, lie, lie,* his brain screamed at him.

"Ah, I'm sorry," he said, feigning disappointment. "She wasn't planning to come. Her family lives around here, so she's visiting with them while I attend the conference."

"Nonsense. Bring her with you! All our spouses will be here, and we'd love to get to know you both on a personal level this week." One of the older brothers smiled widely.

"Well...I don't know." Which circle of hell was this? He fought the shudder that wanted to rip through his body at the thought of what bringing Tweedle Dee to the most important pitch of his life would look like.

"It's important to us that we build relationships with the people we work with," the other brother chimed in.

Jack swallowed.

"He would love to bring Kelly. Right, Jack?" Dan pressed his lips into a firm line. *Figure this shit out.* The decree was communicated as clearly as if his boss had spoken the words aloud.

"Yeah, I'll talk to her. Shouldn't be a problem." The lie floated off his lips.

How the fuck could he make this work? He'd offer her some cash as compensation, and maybe she could make an appearance for a day or two. Then he could send her on her clueless, merry way. Yes. He could pull that off. No matter how much it cost him.

KELLY WASHED her hands for the second time, watching the mucky water swirling in the sink. She'd rinsed her hair and squeezed it out before she soaked a washcloth with warm water. The white fabric took on a dusky brown as she dabbed at the bottoms of her jeans and shoes to get the mud off. She loved these heels, and buying another pair wasn't in the budget this month. Maybe not *ever*.

It was all as good as it would get. She sighed. Ruining her clothes hadn't been her plan for today. She'd only wanted to pay for the gas she'd used to drive to Asheville. But there was no use obsessing about it.

Exiting the small bathroom that barely fit the toilet, sink, and tub, she found Jack pacing in front of the one bed.

He swung his gaze to her and huffed. "Didn't I tell you not to move?"

"Sorry. I'm not up for wetting my pants today." She shrugged, unsurprised by his anger. It was on-brand for the cranky man.

"Well, your small bladder has backed us into a corner." He

scrubbed a hand down his face. "You have to come with me to this conference."

"What conference?"

The breath he let out was long and exasperated. Then he went into a long, boring speech about sports drinks and pitches and advertisers and retailers.

"Stop." Kelly held out a hand. Why did he always make everything so complicated? "Basically, you're saying that the biggest sports drink companies host a long weekend away, in hopes that they'll get better shelf space in their stores or click rates? And companies like yours go to try to form bonds with both the retailers and the brands?"

Jack blinked twice before his brows pulled together. "Yes. You understand that?"

"Of course." Why he thought it was a hard concept made no sense. "But I don't get what it has to do with me."

He shook his head. "They think you're my fiancée."

She tilted her head to the side. "Your *what*?"

With a sigh, he rubbed his brow with his fingers. "Fiancée is the term used for someone you're going to marry." He used the same stick-up-his-butt tone he'd used to explain the umbrella.

But seriously, did he honestly think she didn't know basic words? She crossed her arms. "You really are something else. I know the term; I just don't understand why they would apply it to me."

"Because you're here, in my hotel room." He huffed out a breath. "Thus, I need you to come with me and pretend we're engaged for a few days."

She stared at him, waiting for him to admit that he was joking. When he didn't, she asked, "What kind of ass backward company do you work for? A half hour ago, I was a hooker for coming into the room with you, and now I must be marrying you? This is, like, literally *The Twilight Zone*."

Taking a quick step toward her, he blurted, "I'll pay you. A thousand dollars a day."

Her mouth fell open. "That's ridiculous."

With his eyes locked on her, he took a deep breath. His demeanor changed in an instant, like he'd flipped a switch. A calm settled over him, and a smile that Kelly didn't trust for a second lifted his lips.

What the heck?

"Fine," he said smoothly. "Fifteen hundred a day. The resort's gorgeous, there's a spa, and the food will be wonderful. All you have to do is hang out and pretend we're engaged. Think of it like a mini vacation."

She *could* use a vacation. Plus, not only would a few thousand dollars pay off her credit card debt, but it would buy new shoes, *and* help her get a bit ahead. She might not need to Uber as much. It could make the vacation her roommate and bestie, Cece, wanted to take in May a reality.

"Getting paid to be pampered for a few days. Doesn't that sound ideal?" Jack asked.

"I'd need to go home for a day or so and get organized."

"Out of the question," he said. "We need to be there tonight."

"I don't have clothes. Or makeup. My hair has mud in it!"

"I know we're in Bumblefuck, USA, but stores must exist here too." Charming smile still plastered to his face, he watched her.

"Yeah." She sighed in defeat. "But I can't afford everything I would need when I have perfectly good stuff—"

"I'll buy it. Whatever you need."

"You're going to buy me clothes and shoes and whatever I need *and* pay me to hang out with you?"

"Yes."

She opened her mouth, ready to tell him how ridiculous he was being, when she caught sight of his briefcase. Designer. Her gaze tracked over his suit—tailored to fit perfectly and probably cost more than her rent. His shoes—once again, designer. She remembered the flash of the watch from earlier.

"*Pretty Woman*." She shook her head. She wasn't living in the nursery rhyme about Jack and Jill. She was in a movie.

"*What*?" Jack's eye twitched, breaking the calm façade he wore. Instead of ignoring it this time, he pressed his fingers into his cheek.

"I'm literally in a movie right now."

Jack scowled. "Do you know the definition of literally, crazy girl?"

She rolled her eyes. He could call her crazy, but out of the two of them, he definitely was winning the loony tune contest. "Yes, it means, like, *ridiculously very*. Probably the same thing as epo-whatever."

Jack collapsed onto the bed and dropped his face into his hands. "I am so fucking screwed," he cried, his words muffled.

"Why?"

Elbows on knees, Jack glanced up, looking defeated. "I need this weekend to go well because six months ago I... had a little incident."

"What kind of *incident*?"

"I accidentally slept with a client's wife." He sighed.

How could one accidentally sleep with another person? What kind of a dumbass was this guy?

"*Accidentally*." She rolled her eyes. "What did you do, trip and fall into her vagina?"

"*What*? No, of course not. I just didn't know she was my client's wife until the next morning. And now I'm working hard to get rid of the reputation that misunderstanding created."

"So your boss thinks you're a man whore." Kelly chuckled.

Jack gave a clipped nod. "Exactly. And that's why I can't be in a random motel room with a gorgeous woman who isn't my fiancée."

Her heart stuttered. *Gorgeous*? A blush heated her cheeks. The sexy man in the designer suit thought that she—hot mess covered in mud—was gorgeous?

"Kelly?" he called.

She blinked herself back into the moment. "Huh?"

He closed his eyes for a long moment before scrutinizing her. "Please try to focus for one fucking minute. I need to win this account and prove myself."

Why? The guy obviously wasn't hurting for money.

"Do you even need this job?"

"Not in the traditional sense." Jack rubbed his hand along his smooth jaw. "But it's my father's company, and he's been grooming me to take over for my entire life. He expects me to rise up through the ranks and then replace him one day. But I fucked it all up. And I don't want to be a disappointment."

The words hit her hard, and she brought a hand to her abdomen to ease the pain. There was no way Jack could know how his struggle resonated with her. She'd experienced the same type of disappointment more than most in her life.

"Fine, you twisted my arm," she said before she could think better of it. Her sisters would have a field day with this. They always gave her a hard time for being too trusting. What kind of rational person agreed to go away for days with a stranger?

His eyes widened, and his mouth dropped open, but he looked as though she'd left him speechless. Which was perfect— maybe then he wouldn't ask why. Because she didn't want to explain how much of a disappointment she was to her own family.

"It has to be better than driving strangers around. I'm *so* done with that," she added quickly.

Jack chuckled. "That's good, cause you suck at it."

She rolled her eyes. "Whatever. Could we add dinner into the plan for the next hour? I'm *literally* starving."

"You're not literally starving. You're just hungry."

"No, I'm definitely literally starving. Like, super-duper very starving."

Jack sighed. "You need a vocabulary lesson."

This was going to be a long few days.

7

JACK SCRUTINIZED the man who returned Kelly's wave as he pulled out of the motel parking lot. How could her boyfriend not care that he'd found her at a shady motel with a random guy? But he'd brought her a full gas can and didn't bat an eye when she explained the day's events. It said a lot about Kelly that the guy didn't ask a single question. Not even *how* she'd managed to run out of gas. Jack almost felt sorry for the poor schmuck. Almost. But the sentiment was dampened by another emotion warring inside him.

He tried to ignore it as they got into Kelly's car and pulled back onto the highway.

"He's too old." Shit. Why had he said that?

"To bring me gas?" She raised a brow at him. "He's not, like, so old he can't walk or anything."

A small crease formed between her eyes, and his hand twitched, but he fought the absurd urge to reach over and rub it away.

He clenched his teeth. He would *not* touch this woman. "To date."

She smirked. "*Oh.*" She bobbed her head. "Probably." In a

motion he couldn't help but watch with rapt attention, she released the wheel to tuck her long, thick brown hair over her shoulder, exposing the smooth skin of her neck.

He cleared his throat and forced himself to focus on the way the wipers flicked back and forth. The rain was slowing a bit. Silence stretched between them as he waited for her to elaborate. When she didn't, he couldn't stop himself. "Then why are you dating him?"

"Dating who?"

There went the damn eye twitch again.

"The guy in his forties who just showed up to bring you gas."

Her head whipped in his direction, her eyes wide. "*Eww,* I'm not dating him. That's gross." She turned back to the road. "He's my brother-in-law, and he's known me since I was five."

"Oh." He chuckled. They probably needed to talk about the basics so he didn't make a mistake like that once they arrived at the conference. Other than that she was young, gorgeous, had the vocabulary of a sixteen-year-old, and made his head hurt, he knew nothing about her. But before he could ask his first question, Kelly pulled into a gas station.

Jack unbuckled his seat belt when she parked next to the pump. "I got it."

Kelly gaped at him. "Really?"

"You don't have a coat, remember?"

"Well, yeah. Just *don't* fill it up. Get like twenty bucks."

He froze halfway out of the car and turned to her. "Why would I do that?"

She shrugged, and that tiny crease between her brows appeared again. "Well." She sighed. "Gas is expensive, Mr. Moneybags. I can't afford to fill up. So I just do small doses to keep this baby running." She smiled and patted the dashboard like the hunk of junk was her pet.

"Small doses? *That* is why you ran out of gas. And although

33

you might do it regularly, once in a lifetime is enough for me." Jack pulled his wallet from his back pocket and held up a credit card. "I've got it covered."

"Umm." She tipped her head to the side and opened her mouth but slammed it shut again before uttering a sound. With her hands on the steering wheel, she tapped her nails. Finally, she said, "*Pretty Woman.*"

If she lost the conversation again, he'd lose his shit. "*What?*"

"It means you can pay for the gas." She flashed him a gorgeous smile that might have been more appealing if his eye wasn't twitching at her nonsense. He slammed the door with more force than necessary, but he needed an outlet for his frustration. She was maddening.

Five minutes in the cold, wet night calmed his frayed nerves, and then they were back on the road. If they made good time, they could check in before nine. But that dream died when Kelly veered off the road again. This time into a McDonald's parking lot.

"What are you doing?" The woman couldn't possibly need to pee again. She'd gone during his conference call.

"I told you I was starving, and that was almost an hour ago." She pouted, her plump bottom lip sticking out.

"We'll get food at the resort." He chuckled.

"By the time I stop by my apartment—"

His laughter died, and he frowned. "We agreed that I'd buy you everything you need."

"No, I said I'd come with you, not that I'd let you buy stuff I already have at home. And some stuff isn't replaceable." Kelly didn't even look at him as she pulled into the drive-through lane.

"What kinds of things can't we find at the damn store?"

"My Morphi eye shadow pallet, for one." She said it as though it should be obvious, then went on before he could comment about the ridiculousness of that statement. "And we'll never find my birth control pills on aisle three at Target. Plus, grabbing my stuff at my apartment ten minutes away is so much faster than taking me shopping." She rolled her eyes. Okay, the last two points were valid.

She pressed the button that lowered her window and studied him. "What do you want?"

"I'm not eating this crap." He couldn't remember the last time he'd eaten fast food. Maybe his freshman year of college? That was fifteen years ago.

"Suit yourself." She shrugged. "You can starve, but I don't have to."

After another fifteen minutes, because Bumblefuck backwoods didn't understand the concept of *fast* food, they were on the road again. Now it was time for their chat. He popped a fry into his mouth and turned to his companion, who huffed out a laugh.

"What?"

"I'm glad I ordered extra. My nephew does this crap all the time."

"Does what?" He grabbed another fry. He'd forgotten how addictive these things were.

"He eats my food after he tells me he's not hungry."

Shrugging, he said, "They smell really good." He sighed, working up the mental fortitude he'd need for the coming conversation. "We should talk about some basic stuff so if people ask, we'll be on the same page."

"Like allergies and medical conditions?"

What? "*No*, like how we met, how long we've been together —things that might come up in conversation."

"Oh." She pinched her forefinger and thumb together until they almost touched. "Just *one* little problem."

That twitch was back. He reached for his right cheek in an

attempt to make it stop. "What?" He bit the word out, knowing his tone was harsher than necessary.

"I do better off the cuff. I'm never going to remember what we come up with, and even if I do, I'll probably go on a tangent and off script anyway. So we should just roll the dice and see what I say." She flung a hand in the air.

He ran through every outlandish scenario she might come up with. His job, his career, and his father's respect were cradled in this woman's hands. This woman, who liked small doses of gasoline, didn't believe coats were required, and offered to be a hooker after receiving a compliment. "I am so screwed."

"You worry too much. Anyone ever told you that?"

No, he couldn't say he'd heard that before. Admittedly, he had people who took care of things for him. Assistants, cleaning staff, drivers. Running out of gas wasn't a thing because Stan would be fired if that happened. And yet here in Bumblefuck, with his little Tweedle Dee, every worry became a very real possibility.

When they entered her apartment, he held his breath, expecting to be confronted with total chaos. But the space was neat. There was no clutter or mess, and it was feminine, but in a minimalistic way. Shockingly, her couch wasn't covered with sixteen throw pillows, and the surfaces in the living area weren't cluttered with a million picture frames.

"This is"—he turned in a full circle, taking in the small space—"nice. Do you have a cleaning lady or something?"

His place in LA wasn't even this neat.

"Are you kidding me?" She glowered in his direction before she huffed. "What about everything you've seen makes you think I could afford a cleaning lady?"

Yeah, he'd give her that.

She went on before he could respond. "You and I are in two totally different tax brackets. At the rate I'm going, my next career option might be cleaning houses. It can't be as bad as nursing."

Had this crazy girl been a *nurse*? "*What*?"

"Nothing, never mind." She flung a hand out, her burgundy nail polish a crimson slash in the air. "Bottom line. I would *be* the maid long before I'd be the one hiring the maid."

Without preamble, she headed toward the back of the apartment. He followed her through the open-concept space, smirking at the bookshelf in her bedroom which was, predictably, full of stuffed animals but didn't contain a single book.

"I know," she waved a dismissive hand at the bookcase before he could voice his criticism, "but my dad used to get me stuffed bears for Valentine's Day every year." The little dent appeared between her brows, but she shook her head and strode into the bathroom. "It used to be our thing."

"Used to?" A pit of unease opened up in his gut. *Had he passed away?*

"We're not in the best place." She cleared her throat, and the tightness in her voice made it clear he'd hit a nerve. She appeared in the doorway, then moved past her desk. Against the wall there, he caught sight of a line of books. *Modern Quantum Chemistry, Twilight, Ice Plant Barbarians, Our World in Elements, Balancing Chemical Equations, The Selection.* Her tastes were oddly eclectic.

She dug through a small dish on the dresser that sat adjacent to the desk, then pulled out what looked like a ring. "Want me to wear this?"

"What's that?" he asked.

"It's my *I'm going out, but I want to be left alone* fake engagement ring. It keeps the jerks away."

He blinked. "What?"

"You know that women sometimes pretend to be in relationships to keep the creepers away, right?" She slipped it onto her finger.

That was a thing? He opened his mouth to ask her to elaborate, but he was cut off by a voice echoing down the hall.

"Hey, chic-a! I'm home and in need of some wine and maybe an IV. Although I should have coffee because I have ten more hours of work." A tall blonde froze at the threshold of Kelly's room and cocked her head to the side before peering around him at Kelly. "Do I *want* to know?"

If he hadn't been the topic of conversation, Jack might have laughed at the incredulous tone she used. This woman had clearly been dealing with Kelly for a while.

"No," Kelly said. "But I'm going away for a few days."

The blonde pressed her lips into a tight line and crossed her arms over her chest. "Define away."

Kelly headed back into the bathroom before calling out. "He's pretty womaning me for the weekend."

"Holy shit." The blonde turned her glare on Jack. "I know you're strapped for money, but seriously, Kel. Prostitution isn't the answer."

Jack's eyes widened. "*What?*" He darted a panicked look at Kelly, who dumped an armload of god knew what into her bag.

"Don't make it weird." Kelly rolled her eyes as she finally gave them her attention. "The movie wasn't about prostitution." She paused. "Well, I mean it *was*, but it was about how he needed a date for a weekend, and he paid her a shit ton of money to do it."

Huh. That tracked.

"Can I see you a minute, please?" The blonde gestured to the room across the hall.

Kelly rolled her eyes again before heading in. Then the blonde slammed the door behind them.

Jack rocked back on his heels and perused the room as the women conferred across the hall in tones he couldn't make out.

Above her bed hung four black picture frames. Each looked like a diagram of a molecule, but they were labeled chocolate, serotonin, dopamine, and caffeine. He turned to the desk to look at the books again, but he paused on the painting. It was a landscape, a print of a Thomas Cole. He had the same one in his office.

Odd. Looked like they had similar taste in art.

Finally, Kelly reappeared and shut the door gently behind her.

"All settled." She smiled and moved to the bed.

With his hands on his hips, he watched as she threw stuff onto the bright-colored duvet. When she tossed the bras and panties into her bag, he tensed. Fuck. And without wanting too, he pictured all of those fine curves covered in nothing but black lace. Thoughts of throwing her on the bed flooded his mind. He cursed under his breath. This had nothing to do with the *Pretty Woman* prostitution nonsense she kept spouting. This was a business deal.

And he needed to keep his head in the game.

8

OF COURSE THE resort had a freaking valet. Why would she expect anything less? The need to remember how different he was became more pressing every minute. Cece's parting words echoed through her mind—*this has disaster written all over it.* But Kelly refused to believe that. She'd make this work.

She handed over her keys to the valet, who couldn't have been more than eighteen, knowing it was probably the crappiest car the kid had ever parked. Ninety percent of the cars in the lot were Beemers or Mercedes. There wasn't another Kia in sight.

"Babe?"

Jack didn't seem at all embarrassed by the car. He had gotten out and nodded at the kid. Then he'd grabbed their bags like nothing was out of the norm. But he must have thoughts, because the man was disgusted by cheap motels and turned his nose up at fast food. Not to mention the confusion on his face at the idea of her being a maid.

But she *could* clean and declutter pretty well, so maybe it wasn't a horrible idea.

"Babe?"

The building was gorgeous. It was brick, with large white

columns and windows that made it look like it belonged in a fairy tale.

"*Babe*?"

She had heard Jack say it a few times, but at no point did she think he was calling her. Turning her focus back to him, she realized that he'd been trying to get her attention. But why was he calling her babe?

Oh, pet names. Right.

"I prefer pooky bear." She smiled, watching his right eye tic and his mouth fall open in horror. "I'm kidding." She laughed.

"I'm going to die of a brain aneurysm," he snapped, picking up both of their bags.

"I'm leaning toward old age. Peacefully in my sleep."

He froze and spun to face her. "*What*?"

"Were we not discussing how we wanted to die?" she asked. Geez. He was the one who'd brought it up.

"No." The words escaped through gritted teeth as his eye twitched again. "We weren't. Let's go." He tipped his chin in the direction of the glass doors.

The open area in the center of the resort looked like something out of a movie. It was like a garden oasis with fountains and large plush sofas scattered around. The middle was open all the way up to the glass ceiling, with several levels of balconies lining the edges.

She shook herself, then hurried to follow Jack to the concierge desk. Since he was a bit high-strung, it was probably best not to keep him waiting. She stepped up as the guy handed him keycards and confirmed a room number. A *single* room number.

"Wait, aren't we getting two rooms?" she interjected.

Jack spun slowly to face her, his eyes wide. "No, *babe*. Why would we do something like that?"

She bit back a yelp as he bumped her foot with his toe, his eyes pleading with her.

Oh. *Oh.*

"Just kidding with you, *pooky bear*." She shot him a wink.

He groaned before signing a piece of paper.

As they headed for the elevators, she took a deep breath and opened her mouth—

"No."

His command snapped through her, and she swallowed hard. He might be pissed, but angry Jack was hot. She'd always had a thing for a bossy dude.

That zing in her stomach didn't subside as she studied him in the elevator. Even through the suit, she could see his shoulder muscles bunch as he adjusted his briefcase. Sharp green eyes stared ahead. His jaw was clenched, but boy, was it chiseled. Tall, broad shoulders, quite a package. She leaned back and craned her neck.

"What are you doing?"

She smirked. "Checking out your ass."

He sputtered, the action turning into a cough.

"It's so tight." She went on, unfazed by his ability to choke on air. "I bet you could bounce a quarter off it. People in such good shape are annoying."

Wide green eyes swung her way. "What?"

"My ass will never bounce a quarter, and I'm woman enough to admit it makes me jealous." She owned her curves, but *tight* was something she'd never be.

Before he could respond, the elevator dinged, and he held his arm out, signaling for her to go ahead of him.

"Don't watch my ass jiggle."

He chuckled darkly and leaned in. "Crazy girl." His breath bounced off her neck, and she fought the shiver. "I've been watching your ass since the first time you stepped out of your car."

She froze, at a loss for words for possibly the first time in her life. But he just laughed harder. Jerk. So she lifted her chin and walked out. Her stunned silence continued as they entered their suite. It was bigger than her entire apartment, with a full kitchen and sitting area decked out in high-end furniture and fixtures.

Yup, she was definitely in *Pretty Woman*. Except she wasn't Julia Roberts. She was just Kelly Jillian. She looked down at herself. Jeans, half covered in mud, basic T-shirt. Yup, she was way out of her element.

"I need a shower." She needed to feel less gross. Now.

"Okay, I'll order room service."

"We just ate," Kelly reminded him.

"A handful of your fries doesn't qualify as a meal. Anything specific you want?"

Who was she to disagree?

"Maybe something sweet? You pick."

He gave her a curt nod, and she turned toward the bedroom. When she stepped over the threshold, the corner of the bed came into view. The *only* bed. Frozen to the spot, she peeked in. Oh, the bed was huge. They'd make it work. Seven people could sleep in it.

"Don't worry, I'll sleep on the couch," he called from behind her.

Ugh. Now she felt even more disgusting. Was the thought of sharing a bed the size of a football field with her that repulsive? She turned back to the living room, her focus landing on the tiny sofa across the space.

"Which half of you?" She crossed her arms.

"What?" He blinked, his attention darting to her chest before he tore it away again and swallowed thickly. She would feel good about him staring at her boobs, except he'd rather turn himself into a contortionist to fit on the tiny sofa than sleep in the same space as her.

"Which half of your body is sleeping on that small couch?"

she asked, pointing to it. "It's a king-size bed. We can share it without a problem."

"No," he snapped again, but this time, the words didn't send a shiver down her spine. "That's *not* an option."

Good to know he was, in fact, repulsed by her.

"Fine, whatever. I can take the couch. I'll fit on it better than you will." With a shake of her head, she grabbed her suitcase and headed to the bathroom off the living area. If he didn't want to share a bed, there was no doubt he'd be weird about sharing the master bath too.

The shower felt amazing, especially with two shower heads. Her long hair was almost dry when her phone rang on the bathroom counter.

Seeing Ashley's name pop up, she turned off the blow dryer and swiped right to answer the call.

"Hey," Kelly said, hitting the Speaker icon.

"Everything go okay?"

Kelly paused. Oh shit. Had she forgotten a catering thing tonight?

"With, uh—what?"

A long rush of air came through the phone. Talking to Ashley sometimes felt like talking to one of her sisters. Lots of sighs.

"At the bakery," another voice echoed in the background.

Oh, the bakery. Kelly had forgotten she'd been there only this morning. It felt like a lifetime ago.

"Oh. yeah."

Jackson, Ashley's boyfriend, said something she couldn't understand in the background again.

"Jackson wants to know if you brought any cupcakes back for him."

"Actually, I'm—"

But Ashley cut her off. This happened all the time. The two of them had full conversations while Kelly was on the phone. It meant she'd have to keep track of what she'd been saying before the interruption.

Did I bring cupcakes, did I bring cupcakes, did I bring cupcakes.

"I don't know. Why don't you just put the other ear bud in and talk to her yourself?"

She chuckled. This was the way it always went with these two.

Did I bring cupcakes, did I bring cupcakes, did I bring cupcakes.

"Sorry, Kelly. What were you saying?"

"I didn't bring cupcakes because I'm, uh, staying with a friend for a few days near the city."

"Oh, that's nice."

She dropped her shoulders in relief. She could count on Ashley not to ask questions.

"Have a good time, and I'll see you Sunday for the event."

Kelly stared at herself in the mirror, noting the way her eyes widened comically. Oh shit. The event. "Uh, yeah. See you then."

She swallowed. This was so not good. How mad would Jack be when she told him she had to work on Sunday? As much as she wished she could say *Jack is paying me more in a day than you pay me in a week*, her job with Ashley was long term, and this agreement with Jack was a one-off gig.

Before she could turn the hair dryer back on, her phone chimed, alerting her to a new text.

> Cece: Forget to call me or dead in a ditch?

Oh lord. Cece was such a worrier. She'd demanded Kelly check in once they arrived, but Kelly hadn't had a chance yet. She hit Cece's name and waited as the video call connected.

"Oh good, you're not dead," Cece said, her tone deadpan.

"I told you."

Cece frowned.

"Cec, this place is gorgeous. The room is huge, and I'm telling you, this guy is totally above board. It's all good. And this means I can pay for the cruise in May." Kelly smiled as she pulled her hair into a ponytail. "I'm totally good. Have a glass of wine, and we'll chat tomorrow."

"Oh, I'm on glass number two." Cece lifted the long-stemmed glass containing the crimson liquid. "And tomorrow I have hospital hours all day."

Kelly loved chemistry, and she was awesome at math, but she didn't miss dealing with the hospital rules or worse—blood. She shuddered at the memories.

"We were supposed to go over the formulas for prescriptions again tonight." Cece took a sip of wine.

"When I get back, we'll do it. I promise. But I gotta run." Kelly sent off two air kisses and hung up before Cece could argue. She loved the girl, but damn, she needed to chill with a capital *C*.

She headed back into the main room, finding Jack at the rectangular table in the middle of the open space, frozen in place with a fork halfway to his mouth. He looked like a statue of a Greek god. Which one was it? Zeus? Poseidon? Probably Hades. She got the feeling that Jack had a dark side.

He stared at her for so long she looked down to make sure she hadn't forgotten pants.

Finally, he dropped his fork to his plate with a clang and spoke. "Aren't you cold?"

Cold? The place was a sauna. Was he one of those people who was always cold? Maybe that was his deal with coats.

"Not really. But I do have a small problem." She held her index finger and thumb close together.

His jaw clenched, and his eye twitched. He should really have that checked.

"I forgot about work."

His green eyes narrowed. "You have a job? Besides driving an Uber?"

She waved her hand. "Oh yeah, I only do that here and there to make extra cash."

He blinked twice, so she went on.

"I work for a catering company. Didn't I mention that?"

Jack dug his fingers into his temples and moved them in small circles. Did a doctor tell him about the aneurysm thing? Because he did seem to have issues.

"Don't panic," she soothed

That made his jaw clench tighter.

"I'm good until Sunday morning."

His head shot up, and he gaped at her. "Sunday?"

She nodded, giving him a smile.

His shoulders sagged, and his faced relaxed. "That should be fine. We'll say you're going to visit your family for a few days while I finish up here."

Kelly nodded and then scanned the food laid out on the table. "You didn't wait for me?"

"You said you weren't hungry."

"But I said I could go for something sweet. This is probably why you have to fake having a fiancée." Kelly rolled her eyes, then sat at the table and picked at a few things. She had to admit this was a hell of a lot better than McDonald's.

Jack leaned back in his chair and studied her for a minute before speaking again. "I think we should know at least a few things about each other."

"Okay." She shrugged. "But stick to facts. If it's real, there's a better chance I won't forget it. Ask away."

He cocked his head to the side and gave her a questioning look, his fork once again paused in midair.

"You know, like twenty questions? Get to know you style." When he just blinked, she went on. "We'll take turns asking

47

questions." She said each word slowly. Sometimes Jack seemed smart, but other times it was like he was the dullest tool in the shed.

"Fine." He cleared his throat. "Do you have a boyfriend?"

Kelly huffed. "I wouldn't be a very good girlfriend if I agreed to fake date someone while *actually* dating someone else. And what kind of guy wouldn't freak out if his girlfriend said, 'hey I'm hanging out with a hot rich guy, pretending to be his fiancée'?"

Jack smirked. "You didn't answer the question."

"No, I don't. My turn. What's one thing you've had to work for in life rather than have handed to you?"

His forked clinked against the plate as he toyed with his pasta, not meeting her eye. He was quiet for so long she wondered if he wouldn't answer, but finally, he mumbled the words. "My father's respect."

She sucked in a hard breath, his confession slicing deep. She understood more than she could articulate. Upper middle class —that was how her upbringing could be described. She hadn't known what it was to struggle until she finally admitted the smell of blood made her want to pass out. And it had been too late.

She shook her head. This was a turning point for both of them. He was at least ten years older, sure, but neither wanted to be a disappointment anymore.

He cleared his throat and picked his fork up again. "What's your favorite color?"

"Pink."

"Of course." He laughed.

And the questions stayed light after that. He played basketball in high school and joined a frat at Pepperdine University. He'd never lived anywhere but Cali, and her upper middle-class life seemed like the poor house compared to his silver spoon upbringing. Finally, after her third or fourth yawn, he said it was time to turn in.

But after tossing and turning on the small sofa a hundred times, she gave up. The couch was uncomfortable AF. There had to be a better way. She wasn't spending the night sleeping on this stupid, uncomfortable couch. Jack could just get over himself.

9

JACK KICKED the blanket off and spun before punching his pillow. But no matter how many times he adjusted his position, his problem wouldn't go away. He couldn't erase the image of Kelly walking out of the bathroom in that cropped tank top and shorts. For fuck's sake, why couldn't she sleep in sweats? Then again, the woman didn't do coats, so he shouldn't have been surprised by her evening attire.

He yanked the blanket up over his chest and stared at the ceiling. The suite was silent, so Kelly must have fallen asleep. On the other side of the door. In tiny shorts and a crop tank and so much skin. His throat felt thick, and he swallowed hard. He needed to focus on vitamin water and the best way to sell the Hills on the Nickles Group, but the blue-eyed temptress haunted his every thought. So what if she smelled like apples and sin? So fucking what?

Go to sleep.

Dammit. He was so turned on, his body was burning.

This was why he'd shot down the idea of sharing a bed. Although he'd offended her with his refusal, it was the safer option. There was a constant tension in the air between them, and he didn't trust himself to keep his hands off her if she was in bed next to him. But he couldn't spend the night fantasizing about slipping his hand under those itty-bitty shorts and into all her warm heat.

At this rate, he'd be dead on his feet tomorrow. Kicking off the blanket a second time, he sat up. Maybe he'd grab a drink to take the edge off and calm his thoughts.

Moonlight from the large windows that lined the far wall illuminated the open space enough that he could make out a small form lying on the floor.

Not the couch.

Why was she on the fucking floor?

As he stepped closer, he took in the cushions and pillows. The makeshift bed. Fuck, he was an asshole. He'd promised her a vacation at a spa-like resort. But here she was, forced to sleep on the floor like they were on a backwoods camping trip. He knew what he had to do, even if it killed him.

He crouched low and scooped up the curvy brunette—who would surely leave him with a permanent twitch in his eye after this week. She stirred and peered up at him through half-closed eyes.

"What are you doing?" she murmured.

"Taking you to the bed."

"Oh. Good. That couch sucks."

He chuckled but stiffened, the humor he'd felt dying instantaneously, as she lay her head against his chest and relaxed into his hold.

In her peaceful, sleepy state, she seemed so fragile, so unlike the maddening woman who was always too much. He smirked. Right now, she was almost angelic looking. That twisted weird in his gut, and he brushed the thought away, reminding himself that she made him insane.

With the covers pulled back, he laid her on the bed, swallowing hard when her tank slid dangerously low, revealing the swell of her breasts. Damn, she had perfect tits. Full, round, and more than a handful each. This was going to be hell on his control. Her long hair draped across her face, and with a gentle swipe, he brushed it off her cheek.

Beautiful. And a distraction he couldn't afford. He considered heading to the couch, but she was right. He was two feet too large for it, and he refused to sleep on the floor.

Cursing, he adjusted himself and slid into bed next to her.

"I'm cold," Kelly mumbled before rolling toward him.

Probably because she wasn't wearing any damn clothes. He lay frozen, praying she didn't scoot any closer.

When she didn't stir again, he let out a hard breath and relaxed, doing his best to ignore her sweet fruity scent, and drifted off to sleep.

JACK GROANED, his muscles tightening as softness and warmth pressed tight against his painfully hard cock. Was he dreaming? No, this felt too real. He popped his eyes open, taking in his surroundings. Every plane of him was nestled into Kelly's back. His arm was draped around her midsection, and his hand was splayed along her stomach.

Slowly, and with all the precision he possessed, he untangled his legs from hers. She was so soft and warm, and all he really wanted was to tuck his head into her hair and slip back into the peaceful sleep he'd just woken from. Instead, he inched his arm out from behind her head, only to have her roll over and plaster herself along his side, resting her head on his chest.

Worse. This was worse.

Now her silky bare leg was draped over him, and he was very aware of the way her pussy pressed flush against his thigh.

He couldn't remember a time when he'd been this intimate with a woman. Sex, yes, but entwined with one another in sleep? Never. Closing his eyes, he drank in the moment. Her scent enveloped him, and every muscle of his body took notice of where her body made contact with his. He should move, put space between them, but the selfish prick that existed deep inside him enjoyed the shit out of this moment. She shifted, rubbing her cheek into his chest, before a soft moan slipped through her lips.

Fuck. That sound.

She shifted again, and the rub of her hips against him sent every drop of blood in his system straight to his cock. It ached for more. So much more. When she moved again, he pressed along her lower back, holding her tight.

"Jack."

His name on her lips came out as a breathy moan. He prayed she'd call out to him again. Over and over.

Unable to tear his gaze away, he studied her lips, then brought his attention up, meeting blue orbs that looked at him with a mix of surprise and desire.

He angled closer, his subconscious screaming, though he ignored its warning.

She met his advance, molding her lips to his. He let his body take over, cupping her jaw and rolling them so he caged her in and deepened the kiss. Their tongues dueled while she explored his back, her touch featherlight, and he ran his hand down her side and gripped her hip to pull her tighter into him.

When she moaned into his mouth, his brain took over, reminding him of why they couldn't mess up his plan.

10

WHAT THE HELL? One minute, Jack was kissing her like she was the last woman on earth, and in the next, he'd all but jumped out of the bed like she had bitten him—and not in the good way. The pacing and hair grabbing implied this was a disaster, but she didn't see the big deal.

"I've never had a complaint about my morning breath, so what's your problem?" Kelly sat up and pulled her tank top strap back up her shoulder.

"We can't." He paced, his focus on the carpet under his feet. "I can't." He yanked at his hair again. "You're a distraction I can't afford. You can't do this to me."

She rolled her eyes and sighed. "You kissed me! You keep calling me a crazy girl, but I think you're the one with a few screws loose."

Tossing the covers off, she swung her legs over the side of the bed and stood. And with a huff, she stood in front of him, forcing him to stop his pacing. Without her permission, her gaze tracked down his chiseled abs to the top of his mesh shorts. Of course he had an eight pack. It went perfectly with the quarter-bouncing ass.

"You were humping my leg and moaning."

Heat crept up her neck. There was no way. She'd gone to sleep on the floor and vaguely remembered Jack moving her to bed. But the next thing she knew, she was wrapped up in that hot, hard body. And he was dropping his lips to hers.

"Dude, it's not 1910. I could literally walk around naked, and it still wouldn't mean you could kiss me or blame me when you did. Yeah, I kissed you back. But. You. Kissed. Me." She slammed her finger into his chest, emphasizing each word, then stomped past him. With more force than she intended, she slammed the bathroom door, wincing at the vibration.

The buzzing sound from the counter stole her focus. Ahh. *There* was her phone.

> Mom: We may fail when we try, but not trying is always a failure.

Kelly huffed. Her mother and her epic inspirational mumbo jumbo. She clicked over to her best friend's texts.

> Cece: He didn't murder you in the night, right?

> Cece: Kel?

> Cece: You okay?

> Cece: You're dead, aren't you? Should I send my dad and his search and rescue team to scour the woods?

> Kelly: Geez, relax. Your dad and the hot fire boys don't need to come. Like I said yesterday, no one dies in Pretty Woman. I'm fine.

Cece started her rounds at six, so she probably wouldn't

answer for a couple of hours. Kelly set her phone on the marble countertop and picked up her toothbrush. When she emerged, Jack was on the crappy sofa Kelly refused to sleep on again. If he was going to be weird, then he could squish his large ass onto that bumpy shit.

"You're right." Jack bowed his head, his elbows resting on his knees.

"I usually am." Kelly shrugged. She didn't wait for an answer before heading into the room to her suitcase. "What should I wear to this breakfast thing?"

He appeared in the doorway, brows knitted together. "I thought you were mad."

"About breakfast?" Kelly cocked her head. He was paying her to go to stuff. She didn't think she was allowed to get mad about it.

"No, about kissing you."

She glanced up. "No, I was mad 'cause you acted like a dumbass."

"That's what I was saying. You were right, and I was apologizing."

Kelly glanced up. He'd propped himself against the doorjamb, arms crossed, hair going every which way, his thin lips pressed into a tight line.

"Okay. So what do I wear?" She went back to her suitcase. Jeans were probably too casual. But a dress and heels were too much for breakfast, right?

When he didn't respond, she turned her attention back to him.

He hadn't moved. "You're not like anyone I know." The way his face softened when he said it made it sound a compliment.

She'd take it as one. "Thanks."

"Business casual for breakfast. I need to take a quick shower," he said, disappearing into the bathroom.

Wait—what did business casual mean?

Thirty minutes later, after a frustrating conversation about dress codes and their differences and more introductions than she could count, Kelly found herself at a table of ten people, finally falling into easy conversation. Janice Hill and her sister-in-law, Mary, were friendlier than she'd expected. Their family owned the company Jack wanted to impress, so she'd come to breakfast with the intention of making a good impression, but these women made it easy. She'd anticipated formal and cranky, but they were the definition of chillax.

"We're playing racquetball while the menfolk talk business later. Would you like to join us?" Janice asked her.

"Don't you have to go to the meeting?" Kelly asked.

"I avoid them whenever possible. Meetings are the most boring part of the business. My passion is science. I helped patent the formula for our vitamin water."

"Oh, whoa! So you're badass." Kelly nodded and held a fist out to Janice. "I love chemistry."

Jack's stare bored into the side of her head as Janice chuckled but knocked knuckles with Kelly.

"You'll join us then? For racquetball?" The woman smiled.

"Sure! Sounds fun."

After they'd finished breakfast and had said their goodbyes, Jack and Kelly headed back to their room. They had thirty minutes to kill before the meeting started and she had to be at the racquetball court. There was just one problem...

"Hey, Jack?" Kelly asked as the elevator ascended.

"Yeah."

"Uh—what's racquetball?"

11

W<small>HAT IN THE ACTUAL FUCK?</small> First, Kelly didn't own anything that could even remotely be considered business casual. She'd ended up wearing tight-ass leggings to breakfast. Fuck him and his hard-on. Her ass in those black pants was walking temptation. Then she called Janice Hill, a woman who never put her elbows on the table and always wore pearls, a badass and fist bumped her. Now this?

Why was God punishing him?

"You're telling me you have no idea what racquetball is? Yet you agreed to play a game with three of the most important women here this weekend?" Jack dug the heel of his hand into his eye to stop it from twitching.

She shrugged. "Janice said to meet her downstairs at the courts, so I figured it was like basketball or volleyball. But a racket is the thing you use in that other sport with the yellow ball, right? Crap. What's that called?"

He groaned. "Tennis?"

She snapped her finger. "Yes! That's it."

They were so screwed. But maybe... "You've played tennis

before?" he asked, his tone lifting at the end of the sentence hopefully.

"Nope. But I've seen it on TV."

His shoulders sagged. Definitely screwed. "It's sort of like tennis. I'll walk you down to the courts and give you a quick rundown."

"I'll be fine. Fake it till you make it, right?" She adjusted her sweater as it slipped low on her shoulder. "Can I wear leggings?"

He snorted. Other than one dress and a pair of jeans, that was all she'd brought. They'd have to go shopping after all. But first Kelly had to make it through racquetball without ruining his chance with the Hill family.

When they stood outside the court, his last vestiges of hope withered away.

Kelly furrowed a brow and crossed her arms in the middle of the hallway.

"What's wrong?" He braced himself for the ridiculousness he knew she'd spew.

"Why is the door so small?" She tipped forward at the waist.

Without his permission, his eyes snapped from the door to the scoop of her tank top and sports bra. Good God, she had great tits. "This door barely reaches my hip. I'm supposed to go in there?"

He focused on the door again. Some of the newer gyms had courts with glass walls, but traditional racquetball players liked the wooden walls. So, naturally, a resort that catered to old money had nothing new age.

"What am I, Alice?" she asked nonsensically.

"Who?" He blinked.

"You know. Alice."

He shook his head.

"From *Alice in Wonderland*." She laughed and curtsied dramatically.

Fuck. There was no way this wouldn't end in disaster. He

ran his hands through his hair, praying she'd up her acting game when the time came. Otherwise Janice would see through this whole farce.

Without a word, Kelly ducked through the door, letting it slam behind her. Jack stood in the middle of the empty hallway, frozen in indecision. Should he leave her? But what choice did he have? The purpose of playing the role of happy couple this weekend was so he could land the Hill account. He had to go to this meeting.

After he'd gone over the rules and shown her the basics, like how to hold the racket, he left her there. Through the duration of the meeting, even during his pitch, his focus didn't drift far from his crazy fake fiancée. How was it going on the court?

When he finally stepped out of the meeting, he texted Kelly.

> Jack: What happened?

She didn't respond right away, leaving him in what felt like utter hell as he waited almost half an hour for her response.

> Crazy girl: With what?

> Jack: The racquetball game.

> Crazy girl: Well I was a little disappointed when I didn't end up in Wonderland.

A slap to his back startled him as he was rubbing his eye to stop the twitching.

"You okay?" Ken mumbled as he stepped up next to him.

"Yeah, my eye keeps twitching, and I can't seem to get rid of her—I mean *it*."

Ken's brows rose to his hairline, and he chuckled. "They don't get easier, but it's worth it in the end."

He forced his shoulders to relax and actively engaged in conversation with the Hill brothers as they made their way to their table, but all the while, he scanned the room, searching for Kelly.

When he finally found her, he couldn't stop himself from openly appraising her in tight jeans and an off the shoulder sweater. She tossed her head back and laughed. He halted in the middle of the room as he watched her. Not only was she unquestionably beautiful, but there was a lightness about her that few people possessed.

Kelly turned, and their eyes locked. Although the room was crowded and noisy, for that second, it all disappeared. She raised a single brow, and every nerve in his body came alive.

Ken nudged him. "See? You've already forgotten about whatever she did to drive you insane." He huffed a laugh. "That's the magic of a woman."

He forced a smile. Although Ken wasn't wrong, the interaction he'd just had with Kelly was unsettling.

"Yup," Janice's husband, Cliff, agreed. "They drive us to insanity, but we wouldn't want it any other way."

Ken chuckled. "Come on. Their tongues will be wagging if we stay here yapping any longer."

Jack shook his head and followed his companions to the table.

"How was your meeting, babe?" Kelly popped up and pecked his cheek.

He stared at her with wide eyes before quickly schooling his features. "It was good, but I couldn't stop thinking about you."

An "aww, that's so sweet" came from the other side of the table, but he couldn't pull his attention away from the woman in front of him to respond.

The corner of Kelly's mouth turned up in a slight smile before he pulled his gaze away from her.

"How was racquetball?"

"So much fun. I won two out of the three games."

"Youth has its perks," Janice teased.

He fought back a look of surprise at her announcement. That was *not* how he'd seen it playing out. And he hadn't expected to *not* receive an invitation to drinks with the Hills before dinner tonight. But when he discovered they had a brief meeting with another marketing firm scheduled, Jack understood and could appreciate their due diligence in comparing his father's firm to the competition. Though he couldn't help the niggling disappointment.

"What's wrong?" Kelly asked him once they were back in the elevator.

"The Hills are meeting with a competing firm over drinks before dinner. I was hoping for an invite, you know, to size up the competitor."

"Is that at the Sky Top bar?"

He nodded. "Why?"

"Janice invited us. Apparently, she doesn't like the guy's wife. She asked if I could come to chat with her. Like a buffer. I told her it should be fine, but I wanted to check with you."

His breath halted in his lungs, and without a thought, he yanked her to him and planted a kiss smack on her lips. This woman was unlike anyone he'd ever known.

Kelly jerked back. "Are you going to yell at me again?"

"No." He laughed. "I'm thrilled that you scored an invite. Especially with how worried I was about how racquetball would go. By the way, *how* did you win?"

Kelly shrugged, and her blue sweater slipped off her shoulder. His attention lingered on the smooth skin. The dip of her collarbone. The lines of her neck. Words. She was saying words. Ones he was supposed to be listening to.

"—easy to catch on to. I've always been athletic. Played a bunch of different sports in high school. Drove my dad nuts that I couldn't stick with one thing. Hmm...I guess that could explain the nursing school thing."

He was seriously impressed. Not many people could pick up something the first time they tried it. He draped his arm over her shoulder and pulled her close.

"How do you feel about shopping?"

She froze and cocked her head to the side. "Are you going to snap at my hand with a diamond necklace box?"

Lord only knew what his crazy girl was talking about now, but it made him laugh regardless.

12

THIS MAN. He literally didn't look at the cost of anything. She balked at the prices of the designer dresses a couple of times, but Jack just shook his head like she was ridiculous for caring about how much stuff cost. Not only did he not care about the cost, but he didn't complain when she wanted to try things on. He hadn't rushed her at all. And he'd even picked out a few things, including the dress she had on.

She ran her hands down the silky material. This was the definition of curve-hugging. She liked to actually eat food instead of moving it around on her plate, and she wasn't shy about it, but the look on Jack's face as she'd stepped out of the dressing room in this navy blue cocktail dress had made her feel like a goddess.

With her hair and makeup now done, she made her way to the common area of their hotel room. Her breath caught in her throat as she locked eyes with Jack. Her body warmed at the intense way he looked her over. She could feel it across her skin, his open appraisal of her body.

"I want to regret talking you into that one, but damn, I can't," he mumbled before he locked his jaw tight.

"Wait till you see the back. My ass can't bounce a quarter like yours, but it looks *good* in this dress." Wearing a grin, she spun so he could get a good look. She peered over her shoulder just as he groaned and brought his fist to his mouth.

"Come on, let's get down there before I get my priorities mixed up …" He trailed off with a shake of his head and moved toward the door.

She wanted to be annoyed by his comment, but she looked good enough to make this stick-up-his-butt serious man forget that his life revolved around work. And that sent her confidence soaring. Being pretty wasn't the only thing, but it felt good all the same.

Instead of talking, Jack used the elevator ride to fidget with his red tie. It was cute watching his nerves getting the better of him. His shoulders were pulled tight, and his jaw was locked as he put his hand in his pocket and then took it out again. Then he adjusted his tie once more, this time leaving it slightly off center.

She chuckled and stepped close. Jack's eyes shot to hers, but she focused on his tie. The spice of his cologne washed over her, and she angled closer, unable to stop herself from enjoying a deep pull of his essence. He rested a hand on the curve of her hip, the heat of his palm scorching her skin through the thin fabric.

"What"—Jack croaked, his fingers biting into her hip as he cleared his throat—"what are you doing?"

Slowly, she lifted her hands, triggering a shiver from him when the backs of her fingers brushed against the skin above his white shirt. His tongue came out and wet his bottom lip. She imagined doing the same but quickly blinked herself out of her stupor and focused on his throat, mesmerized by the way his Adam's apple bobbed when he swallowed.

"Just straightening you out." She centered the knot of the bright red tie between the lapels of his navy suit. Instead of stepping back, she rested a palm on his smooth cheek. "Don't be nervous, Jack."

The hitch of his breathing echoed in the silent elevator. And like a magnet pulling her, she drifted so close that almost no space existed between them. He dipped his head toward hers, the move causing a thread of desire to pull tight in her stomach.

"Ahem." Startled by the cough behind her, she jumped back and spun toward the open silver doors and the elderly couple waiting somewhat impatiently for them to exit the elevator.

"Sorry." Jack smiled at the couple and guided Kelly through the doors.

The old woman patted his arm and sent Kelly a knowing smile. "I remember what new love is like."

"What?" She glanced over her shoulder at the couple.

The old man was shaking his head in annoyance, and his wife was still smirking.

"Come on, crazy girl." Jack rested a large hand on her lower back and steered her toward the bar. The stupid nickname should have been annoying, and it could definitely be called rude, but somehow, the way he said it, his voice a low rumble, made the term feel *affectionate*.

Just outside the entrance to the bar, Jack paused, tipped his head left and then right, and shook out his shoulders. He was gearing up. But the calm, turned-up smirk and his calculating eyes were all too familiar. This was the look he'd given her when he talked her into this fake dating ordeal. Like a politician about to shake hands with voters.

She frowned and yanked on his arm.

This business deal was important to Jack, but this wasn't going to help him. She'd seen enough of the Hill siblings to know they liked *real*. Not whatever the hell this weirdness was.

"Why are you being weirder than normal?" she asked.

"What?" Jack scanned the hall, his eyes darting back and forth, and lowered his voice. "Shh. What's your issue now?"

"This whole plastic vibe." She waved a hand up and down. "It's just ew." With her nose scrunched, she shook her head.

Jack glared and crossed his arms over his broad chest.

"It's bad. Won't work in there." She pointed to the bar.

He raised a brow, doubting her yet again. "My business face won't work at a business meeting?"

How could she explain this so he'd get it? "The Hills are totally, you know, *Be Real*."

He blinked twice and sighed. "Be real?"

She nodded. "You know, the app."

"You've lost me."

How did he not know Be Real. Like, what?

"You know. You get a notification on your phone, and you snap a selfie. Right then. No, like, *wait a second, I have to change*, or *I gotta do my hair*, or *wow, I'm doing something stupid*. You just put out what you're actually doing that second. Like, you have to *be real*."

He cocked his head, his mouth pulling into a tight line.

"Like TikTok Now, only less lame?" She tried again.

His expression didn't change.

"Wow, you're old." She shook her head. "Do you even TikTok?"

With a deep exhale, he shut his eyes and rubbed at his forehead. "Kelly. Focus."

"On what? Social media?" She looked back at the crowded bar. "Oh. That's right. The Hills. "Yeah, so, the Hills like real. So be Jack." She waved her hand at him again. "Not whatever that weirdo was."

Jack surveyed the bar, and Kelly followed his line of sight.

"I don't know if I can compete with that guy." Jack nodded to where the Hills were standing with a man and a very pregnant woman by his side. "His wife is pregnant."

"What does that have to do with anything?" Kelly asked. "Is one of the job requirements *must have children?*"

Jack scoffed.

"Personally, I think the Hills will hire someone based on their ability to do their job, not their ability to knock up their wife."

Jack opened his mouth and then closed it just as quickly. He frowned, looking from Kelly to the couple and then back to Kelly.

"I'm telling you. *Be real.*"

"Says the woman *pretending* to be my fiancée."

Kelly bit back a laugh. "Yeah, see? You have enough fake to deal with. And for the record, I'm on birth control, so don't get any ideas. I'm willing to help you, but I'll draw the line waaay before getting pregnant."

Jack chuckled, and his shoulders relaxed a bit. "You really think I can get the job just by being myself?"

"No. Have a good pitch and a plan and show them that Jack Nickles is the best man to head the marketing campaign. But not by being a manipulative weirdo. Now, come on." She grabbed his hand and pulled him toward his future clients. She had faith in him, even if he didn't have any in himself.

To Kelly's surprise, he didn't try to pull out that fake smile again. And it didn't take him long to relax as they chatted with Janice and her husband and a few others.

"We've analyzed our findings, but we can't figure out why potassium isn't being absorbed the way it should be." Janice huffed out a frustrated breath.

Ooh, chemistry. Now this was Kelly's thing. "Have you tried—"

Jack nudged her with a gentle elbow to the side.

She couldn't decipher the look he was giving her. His drink wasn't empty, so maybe he had to pee.

Shrugging, she turned back to Janice. "Maybe you could—"

Jack nudged her again. "Kelly," he mumbled, his voice low and harsh, like he was warning her to be quiet.

She didn't get it, though. Chemistry was her strength. He'd had no problem leaving her to her own devices at the racquet-ball court, yet letting her contribute to a conversation about what she'd spent the last several years studying made him nervous.

"For Pete's sake, Jack, let the woman speak," Janice said. "I'd love some feedback. The solution is probably staring me in the face, but I'm just too close to it."

"See?" Kelly shook her head at Jack before turning back to Janice. "What about adding or increasing the amount of magnesium? It'll bond with the potassium and help it absorb."

"I did think that. Our tech assures us we have the right amounts of each." Janice sipped her wine and looked across the room thoughtfully.

Hmm. This was tricky without seeing the formulas. "What's the ratio of calcium to magnesium?"

"You know chemistry?" Janice's eyes widened, and her lips pulled into a smile. "Jack, why didn't you tell us?"

Kelly doubted Jack even knew. "It was my major in college." She shrugged. She could feel Jack's eyes on her, and in her periphery, she caught his look of surprise before he clamped his mouth shut and schooled his expression. "When I got the degree, everyone told me I should be a nurse. But I couldn't do nursing school."

"Why?" Janice asked, her brow furrowed.

Kelly blew out a breath, making her bangs flutter. This part made her seem ridiculous. "Blood. I can't stand the smell of blood." Kelly shuddered.

"You, Miss Jillian, are full of surprises." Janice chuckled and patted Kelly's arm. "Come to the lab with me tomorrow? I would love another set of eyes on this thing. I think my whole team is missing something."

"Sure. Sounds fun. Labs were my favorite part of college." Kelly paused. "Well, besides the parties."

Janice laughed again.

Within minutes, the group made its way to their table for dinner. Kelly followed the crowd contentedly until Jack grabbed her by the elbow and pulled her aside.

"Chemistry?" he asked as he braced one hand against the wall above her head and leaned in.

"What?" Kelly questioned. If he meant the way it echoed between them, then yes, she could feel it too. Even now, her body was humming at how close he stood.

"You have a degree in chemistry?"

"Yeah. Well, biochemistry." She shrugged. "I graduated with honors from UNC Chapel Hill last spring."

Jack's brows were hanging out at his hairline, and his mouth hung open, but he didn't speak.

She pulled her lips together. "I don't see why that's like *oh my god, no way.*"

"Well...it's literally hard to explain how super-duper very, like, totes shocked I am..." Jack trailed off with a chuckle.

"Not everyone who's smart uses big SAT words." She huffed and crossed her arms.

He angled in farther, his breath dancing off her skin. "Very true. And Janice is right—you are full of surprises." The whisper in her ear sent a shiver down her spine. His nose lingered in her hair while he breathed her in. "Come on, Miss Jillian, let's go before this dress distracts me from my primary focus."

"Yes, getting the water contract."

He chuckled. "Jack and Jill went to the Hills to get the water contract."

Her mouth fell open. "I said that first!"

"I know, but at that point, I just thought you were crazy." His gaze burned into her.

"And now?" she asked, breathless.

"I know you are, but I *like* it." He smirked and turned, tugging her by the wrist toward their table.

13

JACK CLENCHED his jaw for what felt like the hundredth time tonight and forced his eyes to stay trained on the elevator doors as they closed. He'd spent too much of the evening distracted by the beautiful brunette in a navy dress. Although the garment wasn't short or cut too low, it clung to her every curve, making her look damn sexy. He felt like his heart stopped every time he looked her way.

What the hell had he been thinking when he convinced her to get *that* dress? How many times over the course of the night had he fantasized about finding a dark corner and dragging that dress up around her waist and—

He glared hard at his reflection again.

"What is your deal?"

He turned toward Kelly and was met with heated eyes, but the flames burning in her irises didn't correlate with the way he felt. He was mad at himself for being so distracted by her. But this? He knew this look. She was pissed at *him*.

"What do you mean?"

"This game of hot and cold. One minute, you want me and

you're practically eye-fucking me from across the room, but in the next, you ice me out."

"I've told you. I can't afford the distraction, and you are one hell of a distraction."

"It's only distracting because we haven't done it yet." She rolled her eyes and continued on as she exited the elevator. "Everyone knows that once you get sex out of the way, it's not a big deal anymore. It loses the appeal."

What kind of guys had she been involved with? If a man didn't leave her begging for more, then the idiot didn't deserve the right to touch her.

"Not if the guy does his job," he huffed.

She spun toward him outside their room so abruptly that he almost crashed into her.

"Let me guess. You think you'll blow my mind so hardcore that I'll never want any cock but yours again? Because," she licked her lips and let out a breathy sigh that echoed straight down his body, "no one will ever make me see stars like you do?" Another little sigh that had his cock twitching.

But then she dropped the act and shook her head. "Please. Everyone with three legs believes that."

He leaned forward, ready to tease her, tempt her, but his reasons for being here rushed back in before he could make a move.

"As much as I'd love nothing more than to accept that challenge, it doesn't matter. I don't have protection with me."

There. She couldn't argue that point.

"Protection?"

"Yeah, you know, *condoms*?" he whispered, doing his best to be considerate of the guests in nearby rooms.

But Kelly wasn't making that same effort. "We already had this conversation, remember? You are *not* knocking me up to prove to the Hills that you can sell vitamin water. And

73

remember how I had to go home to get my birth control pills? Because Target *still* doesn't sell them over the counter?"

"Condoms exist for reasons that have nothing to do with babies too," he hissed.

She cocked her head to the side. Oh, for the love of God. Surely, this woman had heard of STIs. She freaking dropped out of *nursing* school.

He huffed out a sigh. "There are *other* things that people might need protection from when having sex."

"Oh my god. Are you assuming I have an STI?" Her eyes widened and her jaw dropped open for the briefest of moments before the expression reversed. In an instant, she was glaring at him, and her lips were pressed into the tightest line. There might have even been a vein throbbing in the side of her neck, but he couldn't be sure.

"What? No." He held up both hands, palms out, to ward off the idea, but his voiced pitched higher as he tried to defuse the situation. "I mean—*no*." He tried again, his tone more normal this time.

Jesus.

"Good. 'Cause I do not." Then her face softened, and understanding shone in her eyes. But he had no fucking idea what the look was for. "Oh. Oh wow. I suck—you're trying to tell me *you* have an STI."

At the sound of a gasp, Jack scanned the hallway, his attention catching on an older couple entering a room several doors down. Both the man and the woman looked at him with pity swimming in their eyes, and he wished more than anything that the ground would swallow him whole. The couple hurried into their room, and the door slammed shut.

"*No!* I'm good too." He slid the keycard in and pushed open the door. "Get inside. I swear I won't make it through the weekend without that aneurysm."

She walked into the room ahead of him and rolled her eyes. "I can't decide whether you're dramatic about that or whether that eye twitch is really going to kill you. Relaxing would probably help. And if you're good and I'm good, then what's the problem?"

"I—"

"'Cause I still don't see how sex with your fiancée"—she used finger quotes around the last word—"would be a problem." She put her hands on her hips, elbows out. "Newsflash, all the other couples are screwing, and they probably think we're doing the same. Wasn't that the whole point? That they see this as real? I just—"

With three long strides, he closed the space between them. Cupping the back of her head with his hand, he brought her mouth to his, effectively cutting off her rant. The goal was to get her to shut up, but the second her soft lips parted and her tongue glided against the seam of his mouth, nothing but the need heating his blood mattered.

That morning's kiss had played on a loop in his head all day, and he'd convinced himself that he'd embellished the memory. That there was no way the kiss was as good as he'd remembered. But as their tongues collided, he knew he hadn't. Because his body was racked with bolts of lust so strong it felt like an earthquake was shaking the room as he tipped her back and deepened their kiss. He brought his other hand around to the base of her spine, caressing the top of her ass with his fingertips while dominating her mouth.

She broke the kiss and stared up at him with dark, hooded eyes.

"What—" She licked her damp lips, then pressed her teeth into her lower lip. And damn it, he wanted to be the one doing that. "Why'd you do that?"

"So you'd stop talking." He gripped her hips and backed her

up against the large wooden table that sat in the middle of the open space. He wanted her, and he was tired of fighting it. "Because you might be right. Trying so hard to fight this is probably why I'm so distracted."

He brushed his mouth against the shell of her ear, smiling as a shiver ran through her.

"I—" The most intoxicating moan he'd ever heard replaced her words and caused his cock to jump as he sucked on the skin below her ear.

Running his hands down the silky material of the dress to where it stopped mid-thigh, he savored her warmth. When he got to the hem, he ghosted his fingertips across the soft skin of her thigh, then slowly inched the fabric up. "I've imagined doing exactly this all night. Tell me you want this. That you want me as much as I want you."

"Jack, I want you so badly." She trailed her hands up his chest and over his shoulders.

"Good. Get that ass on the table." He smirked and stepped back, tugging his tie back and forth to loosen it. "I'll start with my mouth on your pussy. And I promise it'll leave you begging for my cock."

Kelly arched a brow before lifting herself onto the table. "Do your worst."

"Careful what you wish for, crazy. I never back down from a challenge."

She smirked. "Men who can *do*. Men who can't *talk*."

He chuckled darkly. Yeah, he'd have her pleading for more before their night was over. Even if it was the last thing he did. He rolled and cuffed the sleeves of his dress shirt as Kelly slowly spread her knees apart, revealing lacy purple panties.

Stepping closer so they were only a breath apart, he whispered, "Are you wet for me?"

She nodded, her pupils blown out and her chest heaving.

Desperate to find out for himself, he captured her mouth again and trailed his hands up her silky thighs.

"I need to taste you." He hooked his fingers into the waistband of her thong and pulled the scrap of material down her gorgeous legs, anticipating the moment he'd finally get to throw them over his shoulders.

Without preamble, he dropped to his knees and buried his face between her thighs. She bucked hard as he circled his tongue furiously against her clit. And when he inserted a finger into her wet pussy and she screamed out as waves of pleasure racked her body, he was desperate to feel her wrapped around him.

His need climbed higher at the idea of taking her bare, and he couldn't resist any longer. With his palms planted on either side of her on the tabletop, he hauled himself up and positioned his hips between her legs.

"I've imagined fucking you like this all night." He met her heated gaze with his own.

"Like what?" she panted, her breathing still accelerated.

"Laid out in this dress with nothing underneath." The corner of his lips turned up as he rotated his hips and pressed against her center, the friction pulling a gasp from her.

He'd never been this turned on by a woman's response to him. He wanted her to beg. But more than anything, he wanted to know he was pleasing her. That she was as desperate for him as he was for her.

"Jack..." She arched her hips off the table.

With that small movement, the need to remove the last barrier between them and sink inside her overcame him. He stepped back, popping the buttons down his dress shirt, never taking his eyes off her.

Making quick work of his belt and pants, he freed himself, grinning as Kelly traced the planes of his chest and abs to where he fisted his cock. His muscles tightened instinctively under her scrutiny, but he fought the urge to rush. He liked how her eyes darkened as they raked over his body.

She leaned back on her elbows as he stepped closer and lined himself up with her entrance.

Pausing until she met his gaze, he said, "I'm going to fuck you hard and fast right here, like this." Then he captured her mouth once more before pulling back and inching into her heat. "Then I'm getting you out of this dress so I can spend hours worshipping your body."

She moaned and arched her back as he gripped her hips tightly.

"Please, I need—"

He pushed forward until he was seated deep within her. Her pussy clenched around him, creating the strongest waves of desire he'd ever felt to course through him. Bracing his hands on either side of her, he held himself still and let her adjust to him before pulling all the way out and slamming back in.

She gripped his biceps as he moved, holding him tight and meeting each of his thrusts with her own. But he needed more. Deeper. And he wanted her legs wrapped around his waist. He yanked the material of her dress up until it bunched high above her hips, then grabbed her thighs, coaxing her to loop them around him. *Perfection*. It was the only word that came to mind as she laid herself flat on the table and hooked her ankles over his ass.

He drove into her over and over, feeling her walls gripping him tighter with each thrust until he was sure he wouldn't last much longer.

"Kelly, baby." With a hand between them, he circled her clit. "You need to come. Now."

Her spine bowed off the table and her mouth fell open as her orgasm racked her body. And a second later, he was seeing stars as he followed with his own release.

He couldn't wait to do that again. One taste, and he was

hooked. And two hours later, as he lay naked in bed with her asleep on his chest, he wondered why he'd been so against this.

Kelly was right. They were pretending to be a real couple, so he'd enjoy the gorgeous woman in his arms and hope he'd be less distracted from what he'd come here to do.

14

KELLY STEPPED into the elevator and pressed the eight button until it glowed orange. The smile pulling at her lips couldn't be contained. It wasn't only good sex. Although she didn't want to admit it to Jack, he did leave her begging for more. But spending the morning in the lab with Janice had been amazing. The experience was everything that had been missing in her life for months. Playing with the formulas, working to solve the puzzles created by reactions and byproducts, finding creative solutions—it was the kind of thrill she'd lost after she graduated.

During college, she had been a lab assistant for one of her professor's research projects. Dr. Lunom had tried to get Kelly to come on full time after she graduated, but she'd let people—really, her parents—talk her into nursing school. They told her she was too much of a social butterfly for the solitude of lab work. But nothing about today felt lonely or solitary. In fact, Janice's team was filled with interesting people, and Kelly had fit in well.

It wasn't until she stopped in front of their suite that she thought about a key. Her phone and ID were in her back pocket, but she hadn't taken her purse because she didn't want the hassle of keeping track of it at the lab.

What did Jack say he was doing this morning? If he wasn't in the room, she'd just have to convince the guy at the desk to give her a new key. It wouldn't be the first time she'd been locked out of a hotel room with no plan.

Luckily, the door swung open after her first knock.

Jack leaned a sculpted shoulder against the doorframe, and the sexy smirk he wore flipped her stomach. Wow, this man was *perfection*. "Let me guess, crazy girl. You forgot the key and you didn't think about how you'd get in if I wasn't here?"

Perfection until he opened his mouth.

She pursed her lips and shrugged. "I would have talked the front desk into giving me a new one."

He snaked his hand around the back of her neck and pulled her in for a kiss. It wasn't long, but it left her breathless, nonetheless. With his forehead pressed to hers, he took a shaky breath. Desire spun in the depths of his green eyes, and suddenly, she wanted nothing more than for him to push her up against the door and make her forget her name.

"Later." It was a promise that left Kelly shivering with anticipation.

He stepped back and moved across the room toward the table. Memories from last night swirled in her brain as he settled into a chair at the table where he'd had her laid out and screaming. He sent her a smirk, like he could read her mind. But today, the surface was covered with papers and boards and his laptop. He had a Zoom meeting scheduled with his team in California so they could prep for their final presentation with the Hills.

"Unmuting," Jack warned before hitting a button on his computer.

She glanced at the story boards as Jack jumped back into his meeting, discussing how their best approach and pitch would be to target women who are looking for a healthier low-calorie drink option.

"That's a great idea. I'd totally drink that." The ad sucked her into the drink. "Does it taste good?"

Jack pulled a bottle out of his bag and handed it to her. "Give it a try."

She twisted the cap off and let the liquid hit her tongue. The flavor wasn't overly sweet. It reminded her of lime-infused water.

"Oh, that *is* good." She scanned the ingredients on the label and took another sip. This was the original vitamin water; the new one Janice was working on would have added calcium. She hoped to have it stocked all over the country by midsummer.

"How did it go with all that?" Dan's tinny voice flowing from the computer's speakers caught her attention, and he nodded in her direction.

"It was amazing. Janice showed me around the lab, and I got to work with one of her techs. I think we figured out the problem. But until they run more studies, they won't know for sure." Kelly glanced at the bottle again, pondering the difference in the vitamin levels of this water and the test one.

"*Lab*? You worked *in the lab*?" Dan asked.

Didn't he just ask how the visit went?

"Biochemistry major." Jack smirked. With an outstretched arm, he signaled for her, and when she moved closer, he grabbed her hip and pulled her into him. "Janice wanted her to take on a problem at the lab. The two of them have hit it off."

"Everyone at the lab was sups cool." Kelly took another sip from the bottle.

Dan held his hand up. "I'm lost. I thought she was your Uber driver."

If his boss knew he wasn't really engaged, why did Jack have his arm wrapped around her like they were playing couple?

"Yeah, she was my driver..."

"I'm done with that, though." She hated Ubering, and if today had taught her anything, it was that it was time to stop wasting her life working jobs she hated. "I don't know what I'm going to do. Maybe I'll try cleaning services. I really like cleaning." She shrugged. The man on the screen gaped at her, wide-eyed, so she continued. "I'm in the finding myself stage of life."

"You'll figured it out, babe." Jack smiled and took the vitamin water from her hand. He winked, then brought the bottle to his mouth.

Why was he calling her babe now? Jack continued to watch her with a dopey grin on his face, but his boss and the rest of his team were gawking at them, wearing various *what the hell?* looks.

She shrugged and turned to the breakfast counter where a fruit tray, chicken pasta salad, and a mix of breads were spread out. Stomach growling, she grabbed a plate, ecstatic that he'd had room service bring up lunch. Her phone vibrated on the counter, and she sighed at today's inspirational quote from her mother.

Mom: Failure is an opportunity to start over more intelligently.

She must have heard about how she ran out of gas. Looked like this was her way of hinting that Kelly should stop Ubering. Quitting that job might be the only thing she could do right now to make her parents happy. They hated that side gig. After uncovering the food, she made Jack a plate and placed it on the table next to his computer.

"Are you going to the meet and greet tonight?" Dan asked. "Might be a good idea to network with other companies in attendance."

"Oh—Janice invited us to a dinner party at her house tonight. I figured you'd be okay with me saying yes." Kelly took a bite of the pasta salad. Ooh, it was *good*. Jack smiled, and under the table, he put his warm palm on her thigh.

"You got a personal invite to Janice Hill's home?" Dan asked.

She didn't understand why that was a big deal. Janice said she'd invited a bunch of people over.

"Looks like my girl and I are going to the Hills' for dinner." Jack squeezed her leg again, and suddenly, she didn't care so much about dinner. She'd rather stay in the room. Especially since they only had a few more days together.

15

"I STILL DON'T UNDERSTAND why we needed a driver." Kelly slumped into the leather seat next to him. The swell of her breasts was more defined above the neckline of her short cocktail dress as she crossed her arms. Only his crazy girl would complain about taking a limo to dinner.

"No offense, but there's no way we'd take your car to a formal dinner at Janice Hill's house."

Her plump lips pulled into a sexy little pout. The look made him want to take her right here in the car. Even though he'd just had her. After his Zoom meeting, he'd jumped into the shower with her, and in minutes, he'd had her begging and crying out against the tile as he rocked into her. Just the memory had him inching his hand up her thigh. He wanted her in little dresses like this all the time.

"Don't pout. This way, I'm free to touch you."

He brushed his fingers along the outside of her panties and smiled wickedly when she closed her eyes and let out a muffled moan at the contact.

"Not with the driver here." Her words said no, but her eyes said yes.

He tilted closer so his lips were at her ear, her fruity apple scent crashing over him as he ran his fingers over her one more time. "I could just take these panties off for safekeeping."

She shivered and tightened her legs around his hand, locking it against her. "I'm not going to this party with a post-Jack glow."

He could change her mind, no doubt. But she had a point, and he was working to correct his image. "On the way home, then."

She groaned and yanked his hand from between her legs before whacking him lightly on the arm. Jack relaxed back in his seat, feeling light. Possibly for the first time since he'd gotten on that damn plane to Asheville.

The night went better than he could have dreamed. His only niggle of concern came from the absolute joy that radiated from Janice at Kelly's presence.

"She is a gem." Janice smiled, tipping her chin to where Kelly stood by the bar across the room.

Jack nodded. "One of a kind, that's for sure."

Another woman appeared at Janice's side, stealing her attention, and she gestured to Jack to give her a moment.

Jack took a step back to give them some privacy and let his mind wander. If he landed this account, would the Hills want to keep seeing Kelly? In truth, Jack wouldn't mind seeing her when he was in Asheville. She drove him crazy, but there was so much more to the woman than he'd first given her credit for. And the more he learned about her, the more he liked. She was so different from any woman he'd met in the past.

"Here you go, babe." Kelly held a glass out to him, jarring him back to the moment.

He hadn't realized his glass was empty, but he wasn't surprised that she had picked up on it. She'd been running interference for Janice for the last hour, making it obvious that she knew how to read a room. No wonder Janice wanted her here tonight. There was no way she wouldn't want to have Kelly around after this weekend. That fact was cemented when Janice turned her back on the woman next to her and waved another board member over.

"Bill, this is Kelly Jillian," Janice said when the man approached. "She's the one I was telling you about. From the lab this morning." She smiled at his fake fiancée. "He has some questions for you."

Jack stifled a laugh as the three of them fell into a deep conversation. He picked up on words like calcium and riboflavin, but most of it went right over his head. And from the way the woman on the other side of Janice wandered off, she probably didn't understand the lingo either.

At a lull in the conversation, Kelly turned to him. "Bill, this is my fiancé, Jack."

"Oh, yes. We met yesterday. Ken mentioned your firm having some solid ideas for the new campaign."

"Thanks." Jack nodded as he shook Bill's hand.

"So when's the big day?" Bill asked, gesturing between him and Kelly.

"Oh..."

Damn. This was one of the questions they should have prepped for.

"Oh man, the date was such a tough choice. Between weather and flight costs and Jack's work schedule—so we can book our honeymoon—it's been crazy. And there are *so* many opinions." Kelly laughed. "Whoever said weddings are just about the bride and groom was a liar. But I think we picked the best time for weather in LA. Don't you think, babe?" She smiled serenely at him, and all he could do was nod. "I do worry it'll be too hot. But being on the beach and having the breeze from the ocean should be perfect. I have to pick out our flowers when we get home next week."

She barely took a breath before going on about half a dozen

other random things they still had to do and how excited she was about creating her dream wedding.

When they finally excused themselves, Jack leaned close to her ear and asked, "When did you say the date was? I lost track with all your rambling."

She smirked. "I didn't. That was the point."

Oh *fuck*. That was brilliant. Damn, she'd make a brilliant marketer herself.

By the third time the question had been asked, it was natural to drop into this conversation and follow her lead.

"The fight over honeymoon plans was a nice touch." Kelly smiled at him. "But I actually think Bora Bora would be fun."

Images of her in one of the huts that floated on the cerulean water flooded his mind. Skimpy suits and lots of skin. He could see them there, enjoying every minute of the trip. If they booked soon—He blinked. What the *fuck* was he talking about? They weren't getting married. He shook his head.

"Hey, sexy?" Kelly's voice was unusually low as she tucked up next to him. "Check your pocket."

He slipped his hand into his jacket pocket, his fingers brushing against something satin. Maybe... But it wasn't...His eyes widened.

"Ready to go?" Kelly sank her teeth into her lower lip.

Between that and the way her panties felt between his fingers, there was no way he could refuse.

16

THE SECOND THE door slammed shut, Jack had her pressed against it, her shoulder blades digging into the hard surface as he captured her mouth with his. Of their own volition, her legs encircled his hips. When she locked her ankles at the small of his back, he rocked against her. Whoa, the man could kiss. And tease. He'd spent the limo ride back to the hotel toying with her. Releasing her lips, he tipped her chin up, then pressed his mouth against the pulse in her neck, the sensation causing her to arch into him.

"You're mean." She moaned.

"Me?" he muttered as he kissed his way down to her collarbone. "Who put their *panties* in my pocket at my *business* dinner?"

"Is that a complaint?" She chuckled as his eyes shot to hers.

"Fuck no. Do it every time, and I'll be a happy man."

He stepped back from the door, and she unhooked her ankles so she could slide down to the floor.

"No you don't." Jack growled and yanked her legs back up, settling his hands under her ass.

"Jack, I'm heavy." She sighed.

He pressed her against the door again, regarding her intently. "Let's get one thing straight right now." He lifted a hand to cup her cheek. "Your legs belong wrapped around my waist." His voice was low and dripping with unrestrained desire. He hovered so close his lips ghosted across hers as he spoke. Then, finally, he dropped them to meet hers again. All too soon, he pulled back, swinging her away from the door. "So don't give me that *heavy* shit ever again. I have no problem carrying you."

"That's probably why your ass is tight enough to bounce quarters off."

He chuckled darkly as he brushed his lips against her shoulder and strode into the bathroom. "Exactly, crazy girl."

He set her on the counter and moved toward the massive jetted tub across the room.

"Do I have to stay here and wait for you? Or can I get down?"

"As long as the dress hits the floor as fast as your feet, you can get down."

"In a hurry, Mr. Nickles?" She cocked a brow.

Without responding, he turned the water on in the tub.

She hadn't noticed until that moment that the lights were dimmed, and the room had a romantic vibe going. "Are we taking a bath?" The tub was plenty big enough, but...

He spun back to her, his brow creased. "What's with the tone? Do you have issues with baths?"

"No." She scanned the room again. "But I didn't realize people took baths together in real life. I thought that was more of a romance book thing."

Frowning, Jack stalked toward her until their chests were practically touching, making her look up to maintain eye contact. "You've dated really shitty guys, haven't you?"

Not every guy she dated was bad. Just... "I don't know." She shrugged. "Dorms don't have tubs, and since graduation, I haven't dated much. Just a couple of guys whose apartments didn't have tubs anywhere close to this size."

She shook her head. He really didn't get what life was like for the average person.

"Sometimes I forget how young you are," he said, regarding her with an intensity that made her shiver. "Let me be the first man to spoil you, Kelly."

First? Like she'd ever meet *another* gazillionaire who invited her to spend the week in a hotel room bigger than her apartment. "I'm pretty sure you'll be the only one."

When his eyes flared, she decided she wanted to take care of him too. In her own way. Slowly, she pulled at his tie, loosening it before she moved to the buttons of his dress shirt. With her palms pressed to his warm skin, she explored the planes of his broad chest, moving to his shoulders and sending the white material cascading down his arms until it caught on his wrists. Lifting onto her toes, she kissed him.

"Kel." He groaned. "My arms are stuck."

"Well aware." She smirked against his mouth as she worked his belt and zipper. The water running in the background gave her pause. "One sec." She slid around him and shut it off.

"Really hate the bath idea, huh?" Jack chuckled.

"Shh. We'll do that after."

"After what?"

"After I take care of you." She smiled, and with her hands on his shoulders, she forced him to step back until he was even with the bench at the vanity. She lowered his pants and boxers in one tug. "Sit."

He smirked as he tried to reach for her, but his shirt kept his hands trapped behind his back. "I'm still stuck."

"I know." She pushed on his shoulders until he sat on the bench. His shirt caught under him, holding his arms even tighter at his sides.

"Kel?" he asked, his pupils dilated and his breath ragged.

With a seductive arch of her brow, she lowered herself between his legs until her knees hit the cold tile.

Without looking away, she ran her hands up his calves, letting the curly hair tickle her palms as she slowly moved across the muscles of his inner thighs on either side of her. His cock jutted straight up between his legs, long and thick, the tip glistening. She trailed her thumb along the underside.

With a groan, he said, "Please tell me you're going to suck it, baby." He swallowed as she wrapped her fingers around his length, giving it a firm squeeze.

She tilted forward, swiping her tongue over the smooth tip, tasting him. He bucked off the seat at the contact, his cock twitching in her hand.

"Suck it. Now."

She licked her lips and took his blunt head inside. Swirling her tongue before pulling it deep, her eyes still fixed on his face.

His strong jaw was clenched, and his head was tipped back. The cords of his neck were tight. A power surged through her at the sight. *She* made this man feel that good. Again she took him deep, his length filling her until the tip of his cock brushed the back of her throat.

He groaned her name, dragging out the syllables. The deep timbre sent vibrations through her. He tugged against the sleeves of his shirt desperately, but she continued alternating between licks and sucks before once again taking him to the back of her throat.

"You look so fucking good with your lips around me." He flexed his hips, forcing himself deeper.

She groaned around him, relishing the power she had to make him feel this good. Turning him on turned *her* on. Made her own need pound deep in her core. She pulled back and ran her tongue along him again, then swirled around the tip.

The sound of ripping fabric echoed off the tile before he

slipped a hand under her arms and yanked her up until she was settled on his lap, her dress bunched at her waist.

He slid a hand between them and slipped his fingers into her heat. "Sucking my dick makes you so wet, dirty girl." With one quick movement, he sheathed himself inside her, filling her.

Her breath caught at the delicious friction, and she closed her eyes, savoring the feeling. The fabric of her dress brushed against her skin, sending arcs of electricity through her as he lifted it over her head. When the garment lay in a puddle beside them, he pulled her close. Her nipples rubbed against his chest, and she shuddered. He dropped his head and claimed her mouth, devouring her as he sat fully inside her.

Skin to skin, connected to him so thoroughly, she felt every emotion as if it were magnified.

"Ride me," he growled against her lips.

With her hands looped around his neck, she lifted and rocked against him. He groaned and pulled back, watching her, desire heating his green eyes.

"Yeah, baby, like that."

He brought a hand to her waist and guided her as she moved, lifting his hips to meet her every time.

"Jack," she whimpered, teetering on the edge of pleasure, her lashes fluttering.

"Don't you dare shut your eyes," he ordered. "Look at me. See how good we are together."

Obediently, she locked eyes with him as they met each other thrust for thrust. His green irises flared, and the knot of pleasure inside her tightened and swirled, begging to be set free.

She picked up her speed, unable to look away from him. In turn, he kept his focus on her face, his breath dancing across her lips. His eyes reflected so much emotion: desire, need, and maybe something else. All of it amplifying the flames building inside her.

She whimpered and ground hard against his pelvis.

"I got you, baby." With a hand between them, he swirled his thumb around her clit.

Her legs quivered, and she exploded, waves of pleasure bursting through her over and over in an unstoppable torrent. He shifted, thrusting hard, lifting her higher, making her cry out. He groaned into her neck and locked both arms around her as he came.

Their bodies stayed fused together as they floated down to earth, catching their breath and relaxing into their embrace.

"You're amazing, crazy girl." Jack's words vibrated against her neck.

"You're not so bad yourself." She smiled.

But five minutes later, as the bath water rose around them, her head on his chest and his strong arms wrapped around her, the realization hit. Though this was only a weekend fling, she would never find another man like Jack Nickles.

17

JACK LEFT the meeting confident that he would be closing the deal with the Hills. The Hill siblings and the entire board were impressed. They loved the idea of marketing vitamin water to women.

Reserving a private table in the dining room for lunch had been a stroke of genius, especially now that the pitch had gone so well. He wanted to tell Kelly all about the meeting, and he couldn't do that unless they were alone. He beat her to the table, but her text said she was on her way down. The flash of red had him glancing up in time to see her step up to the hostess stand. The cherry crop sweater clung to her and stopped just above her leggings, exposing a strip of skin he desperately wanted to taste. She turned, and her face lit with the most captivating smile when she saw him.

"So it went good?" she asked when she stepped up to the table.

He cringed.

"What?" She cocked her head to the side, worry creasing her brow.

"Nothing. It went very *well*."

The wrinkle in her brow disappeared instantly as her lips fell into a hard line. "Well and good mean the same thing," she huffed.

He reached out and grabbed her hand, entwining their fingers. "Don't get cranky."

"Don't try to make me talk like the dictionary." She smirked at their joined hands before meeting his eyes once again. "Accept that we talk different languages."

He winced again but decided not to correct her grammar a second time. "Okay." The smile he received in return was worth it.

"So the Hills loved the presentation."

It wasn't a question. All morning, Kelly had assured him that he would crush the meeting. She had total faith in him.

"They're on board with my suggested target audience and my ideas about how to do that. I really think I'll get this account."

She gave his hand a squeeze. "I knew you'd do great."

That unquestionable belief in him did something weird to his chest. It was the same feeling he had when he'd stood in the bathroom, holding her as she told him he'd be the only man to spoil her. Her words twisted and yanked on his heart. He wanted to call it unnerving—it almost was—but it was simultaneously the best feeling he'd ever had. Their connection was unmatchable. And not just in the bedroom. She'd never seen him as a disappointment or a fuck-up. And unlike so many of the women he'd been with over the years, she took an interest in his work. Kelly listened as he talked about the meeting endlessly, not cutting him off to change topics, instead asking questions like she truly cared.

"You know, the whole market to women thing will work for the calcium water coming out too." Kelly tapped her nails on the table. "Do you plan to send them a wrap-up email?"

"Yeah." Jack paused as the waitress dropped off their food.

"Add that to the email. Women always need calcium. It's like eden."

"Eden?" He pursed his lips, racking his brain for energy drinks named Eden. But even knowing the market, he came up blank.

She nodded as she slid a forkful of pasta between her red lips.

"I need a translation, crazy girl." Jack chuckled, but his focus shifted to her mouth. He widened his legs uncomfortably as he tried not to think about how those lips had felt around his cock last night. How was it he could go from having an in-depth conversation about work to wanting to bend her over the table in seconds? He'd never had that with a woman before. It was like he was turned on not only by her body, but by her mind.

The feeling, although foreign, wasn't something he would be ready to let go of in a few days. Before the weekend was over, they'd have to talk about where they would go from here. Hopefully, she'd be open to long distance.

"Did you hear me? It's perfect."

Perfect. Was that what they were?

"Jack? Eden. It means perfect."

Oh. Jack blinked himself back into the conversation. "I should put that in the email." That the ideas he'd pitched could so seamlessly be applied to the Hills' upcoming product was nothing short of providence. "What do you want to do for the rest of the day?" He was riding a wave of exhilaration that would translate perfectly to an afternoon spent in bed.

"I promised Cece I would help her go over drug dosage formulas on FaceTime." She shrugged.

Damn, this woman impressed the heck out of him. She was tutoring her friend—who was working toward a doctorate in math—and brushed it off like it was no big deal.

"Okay, I'll finish up the last few things for the Hill account while you work with her." He kind of liked the idea of working side by side.

"Oh!" Kelly dropped her fork. "I forgot."

Jack braced himself. Sometimes her big exclamations led to small issues or admissions, but other times, they signaled massive problems she should have led with but managed to keep buried until an hour into the conversation. It kept him on his toes, that was for sure.

"Janice moved stuff around for dinner tonight. We're sitting at her table."

"Why?" Janice was the type of woman who always had a reason.

"I didn't ask." She shrugged.

Of course she didn't. Kelly probably didn't realize that it was unlikely that Janice could just shift things around at a national conference like that. Nor would it occur to her that a woman like Janice might have an agenda. As smart as Kelly was, her innocence was almost childlike. And the idea that someone might use or hurt her cut him deep.

"Why are you glaring at me?"

"I'm not. I'm just glad you were my Uber driver." He took her hand in his again.

"I'm pretty sure you said I'm a terrible Uber driver." Kelly laughed.

"Oh, definitely."

The confusion on her face told him that, once again, he wasn't speaking her language. But it didn't matter. Kelly moved on to a new topic almost instantly, and Jack just smiled and tried to keep up.

They finished lunch before heading up to the suite, where she set up for her FaceTime meeting with her roommate and he pulled out his laptop. The experience was even better than he'd expected. He liked seeing her across the table. It wasn't a normal job perk, but it made the boring wrap-up emails to the Hills and his team go much faster.

Jack rubbed his eyes. He needed another cup of coffee. But before he could stand, Kelly appeared at his side, wearing a smile and holding a steaming mug, which she placed on his side of the table. She was still rambling away with Cece as she walked back to her spot across from him. Dumbfounded, he found himself staring at the piping-hot black liquid in the mug. How did she—

He shook his head, reminded yet again of how good she was at reading people. With a glance at his watch, he wondered whether they had enough time to shower together before dinner.

Bringing his coffee cup to his mouth, he could feel her attention on him. From over the rim of the mug, he watched her tap her nails on the table before raising his eyes up to her face. One corner of her mouth lifted, and he wondered if she was thinking the same thing.

18

"Is he in the room?" Cece asked over FaceTime.

"You said to call you back when he wasn't." Kelly spun her hair around the wand and yanked slowly, letting the loose curl pop free. "I'm getting ready for dinner tonight."

"What's he doing?"

Kelly shrugged. "I don't know." They'd showered together, and then he disappeared into the sitting area. "Normally, he sits around in sweats, messing with his phone while I get ready. Did you know he didn't even have TikTok until yesterday?"

"What?"

"I know, right? Who doesn't do TikTok? And now he's analyzing it instead of laughing at videos. He called it the perfect seven-second ad-clip for Gen Z." She shook her head, her curls bouncing. "The guy gives amazing orgasm, but seriously, he's so intense. Could be why he gives good orgasm, though. When he's focused, he's *focused*."

Cece sighed.

"What?" Kelly asked.

"I want to have a serious conversation about the fact that you are now actually sleeping with the man paying you thousands of dollars to spend time with him, and you're laughing about TikTok."

Kelly froze mid-curl and then yanked the wand out so her hair didn't burn. They'd have to talk about that. Taking his money didn't feel right anymore. She tapped her nails on the counter.

"Kel?"

What had she said? Probably something about her being concerned about her safety or Jack being sketchy.

"I told you. He's great."

Jack went out of his way to make her feel seen, and not just that "shit, you look hot" thing guys did. He included her in business conversations and looked for her in a room full of people. Their every interaction was just...natural, easy. She'd never had that before. "I know you think it's sketch, but I swear, Cece. He's by far and away the most respectful, most attentive guy I know."

"You are *so* clueless. Do you hear yourself?" Cece frowned.

"I know you're worried. But seriously, Jack is the kind of guy you'd pick for a friend," Kelly assured her again.

"What happens in two days?" Cece demanded. "Think about a future more than two hours away."

"Hopefully, he gets the account and makes his dad proud. And I have that fundraising event for Ashley." She shrugged.

"Not only are we not on the same page, but we're not even in the same book. I don't understand how you aren't more attached. In one breath, you sound all-in, and the next, you sound like, *eh, whatever*."

"Attached to what?" Kelly asked, finishing her last curl.

"Him." Cece rolled her eyes.

Kelly froze. She wasn't attached to her pretend fiancé, was she? He was hot and caring and smart, sure. He'd totally make some girl happy one day.

That felt weird. Kelly chewed on her lower lip, uneasiness

churning in her gut. The idea that he'd make another girl happy didn't sit right. She frowned. The good news was that Kelly would never meet the woman he finally settled down with because he'd be all the way across the country. And that was a blessing for said woman, because Kelly had the urge to hit the nameless, faceless idea of his future girlfriend.

Cece sighed again. "Okay, I can't make you see this for what I think it is, so I'll see you Sunday night?"

"Yep." Kelly nodded.

By the time she finished her makeup, Jack was fully dressed in his suit and waiting in the common room. The man wore a suit like no other. His broad shoulders and narrow hips worked for him. With one hand in his pocket, the planes of his stomach behind the white button-down were on display. His moss green eyes moved up from his phone, and a smirk danced on his lips.

"You better be careful eye-fucking me like that, Kel. Because if you keep that up, I'll make us late for dinner."

She shivered.

Walking straight to her, Jack held out a hand. When she took it, he tugged her close and pressed his lips tight to hers. Who cared if they were a little late.

Forty-five minutes later, Jack was leading her through the dining room to their table.

"We're not that late," Kelly assured him.

"Even if we were," Jack sent her a grin that flipped her stomach, "it was worth it."

What was it about him that made her feel so much? They wound through the room until finally finding the Hills' table.

Janice smiled at her and stood as they approached. She slid her arm through Kelly's and pulled her toward an empty seat at one end of the table. Jack sat with the men, but his eyes stayed trained on her as he settled.

"So glad you're here. Do you see the woman over my

shoulder who's heading toward us?" Janice whispered. "I don't want to talk to her. Do you think you could put her off?"

"Of course," Kelly said as she pulled back. "What do you need me to do?"

"Tell her you're acting as my assistant this weekend. She needs to schedule a meeting. Just schedule it for anytime next month that works for her."

"Easy enough." Kelly stood and made her way toward the serious-looking woman in a power suit, intercepting her and introducing herself as Janice's temporary assistant.

By the time Kelly was back in her seat, her phone had a notification giving her access to a shared calendar with Janice.

"What's wrong?" Jack said from where he stood behind her chair. His breath on her neck sent a chill down her spine.

"Nothing." She shrugged and added the meeting to the calendar. Before Jack could say more, Janice was at her other side, introducing her to the rest of the table. In addition to the three Hill siblings and their spouses, Brandon, a top-floor executive assistant, and his partner were also seated with them.

"Jack, do you and Kelly golf?" Ken asked while they were waiting for their main courses to be served.

"My father and I play twice a week when we're both in LA." Jack darted a glance at Kelly.

"They only let me come sometimes, because I think golf is supposed to be *fun*. And they find it very important that the white ball gets to the hole quickly," she interjected and then smiled over at Jack.

He shook his head with a little laugh, probably wishing he could call her crazy girl.

Linda, Ken's wife, laughed. "You need to play with me, then."

Ken groaned. "Yeah, the rest of these guys," he tipped his head at his siblings, "they won't play with us anymore."

"Control your wife," Cliff called out in a way that told Kelly it was a running joke.

"The two most important words in any good marriage are," Ken paused dramatically, "yes, dear." The entire table laughed. "You'll learn that quick, Jack."

Jack watched Kelly fingering the end of one of her curls. "I feel that a little more every day." Normally, when Jack focused on her, the look was all heat and desire, and it made her heart pound. But this was different. Almost warm, like a cozy blanket.

"Why don't you two join us tomorrow morning?" Ken suggested. "Maybe we've finally found a couple who can handle Linda and me."

"Sure, sounds good," Jack responded.

Throughout dinner, Brandon was pulled away a few times to deal with business, and Janice asked Kelly to intercept two other executives who wanted to meet with her.

Jack squeezed her hand as she took her seat again. There was something different about him tonight. For a moment, she thought about asking him. Then his eyes lingered on the swell of her breasts, and the air between them was normal again—all sexual tension and lust. She breathed out a sigh as he yanked his attention back to the conversation with the Hill brothers.

"You're almost better at running interference than I am. I didn't think that was possible." Brandon had switched seats with Janice because she was chatting with her sister-in-law.

"What?"

"They bring us assistants along to step in when they don't want to deal with certain people, but Janice is without one this weekend. Tamara just gave her notice. She won't be coming back after maternity leave."

"Oh." No wonder Janice had struggled with help this week.

"But I'm glad it's you and not someone else, because Janice tends to be quick to grab on to someone, and a lot of times, they don't work out."

She could see that. The way Janice had taken to her was almost unbelievable. But truthfully, everyone there seemed to fit well together. Brandon and his partner were easy to talk to, and together, they made her laugh. She loved the entire group.

When dinner was over, Jack got pulled into a conversation with two other men, while she chatted amicably with one of their wives.

Kelly scanned the crowd as she half listened to the conversation around her, pausing when she caught sight of Brandon talking animatedly to Janice. They turned in her direction, still locked in conversation, and when they saw her watching, they quickly yanked their gazes away.

Were they talking about her? Had she messed something up? She hadn't thought so. But the idea that she'd done something dumb to hurt Jack's chances with the Hills flipped her stomach.

19

GOLF WITH KELLY that morning had been a once in a lifetime experience. Only she could hit her ball into a sand trap, smile, and skip off like she *meant* to do it. Then, on the next hole, she'd tee off and land on the green for a birdie.

"Incredible what basic skill and not giving a shit looks like in real time," Ken mumbled after Kelly sent another shot straight down the fairway.

"Even after twenty years and a million golf lessons, I'm not much better." Linda laughed as she took off with Kelly in the golf cart.

He watched them bounce a little too fast down the path, then turned back to Ken.

"It's amazing how a person can unsettle you at the same time they settle you, isn't it?" Ken murmured.

"Much the same way she can make you insane and yet"— Jack chuckled—"you *like* it?"

"Yup." Ken pulled his driver out of his bag in the back of the cart before moving to the tee.

Jack waited for him to tee off and then took his shot.

"Nice." Ken nodded before feminine cackles erupted in the

distance. Ken sighed. "Before we take off and find out what those two are cooking up, I just want to say this. I'm glad you're here with us today. You've exceeded our expectations."

Those words sent pride surging through Jack in a way he couldn't have predicted. All he'd wanted was to wow them. And he had. But so much of the credit belonged to his crazy girl.

"Thanks." Jack smiled. "Does that mean you're going with the Nickles Group?"

Ken barked a laugh. "We'll see."

But after golf and then a lunch with the family, Jack couldn't imagine not getting the account.

A chuckle escaped his mouth as he stood outside the dining room waiting for Kelly. Somehow, she hadn't realized she needed to pee while they were still in the room. No matter how busy or distracted he was, he couldn't miss the fact that his bladder was full. But it didn't surprise him that Kelly could. His phone vibrated in his pocket, and when he pulled it out, his stomach fell through the floor. He swallowed hard. He had pretty much nailed down the Hill account, but if his dad was calling, that could mean something was wrong.

Taking a breath, he answered. "Hey, Dad."

"How are things going?" The older man's tone carried a hint of something Jack couldn't place. His father was holding back. But was it something good or something upsetting? He tightened his grip on the phone, but he cleared his throat.

"Good, good." He affected an easy tone. "I think they're almost ready to sign."

He pinched his eyes closed and prayed that was the case.

"I spoke with Ken a little while ago. He's very impressed with you," he paused for a long moment that had Jack's heart rate accelerating, "and your *fiancée*."

Oh shit. He could hear all the questions and skepticism rolled into that one word.

"It's a long story. I can fill you in when I get home," Jack said, not entirely sure how he'd explain Kelly to his father. Because what had started out as a ridiculous mistake had quickly become something so much more.

"I think your mom needs to meet her *well* before she hears the word fiancée."

Jack winced. His mother would probably cry if she thought Jack had proposed to a woman she'd never met.

"Yes, Dad."

"Sounds like Ken was blown away by her."

The Hills all loved his girl. And how could they not?

"Maybe she'll come out to LA with me for a weekend." Jack scanned his surroundings, searching for her, but she wasn't out of the bathroom yet.

He could see her loving LA, and she'd be all bubbly about taking in the sights while grumbling over how much things cost. They'd have to talk about how they'd make long distance work when he went back to California. Maybe she'd eventually be open to moving.

"That'd be nice. We'll touch base once you have everything there wrapped up." A shuffling came through the phone before his dad spoke again. "Proud of you, son."

A knot that he didn't know had been lodged in his chest loosened with those words. He hadn't realized how much he needed to hear those words. Or how desperately he longed to *earn* them.

"Thanks, Dad."

Once he hung up, he smiled at the gorgeous woman who was making her way toward him. The way she smiled back did funny things to his chest.

Kelly gasped when he grabbed her by the hips and pulled her against him. He crushed his mouth to hers, loving how she melted into him when he embraced her and kissed her like this. She pulled back, wearing a dreamy expression.

When Bill snagged Jack's attention, Kelly stepped back to let them chat. But even as he talked to Bill, part of his focus stayed with her. She rarely frowned, so the look on her face and the way she was typing away furiously had him excusing himself and heading back to her.

"Everything okay?"

"Yeah...It's just this guy I hook up with sometimes."

Jack froze. What the fuck?

"He wants to meet up next week. But I—"

"*What*? You're making plans with some random guy? You're engaged." His heart rate spiked, and his fisted hands throbbed because he was squeezing them so tightly. He took a deep breath in hopes of calming himself, but this felt like a monster was trying to break out of his chest and eviscerate anyone who had the gall to be near his girl.

He took a second calming breath, but now she was looking at him with fury in her eyes and her brows pulled together tight.

"We're not *actually* engaged."

Right. They weren't—but still. There was something between them. Surely, she felt it too. But by the looks of her bewildered expression, maybe she *didn't*.

20

WHAT THE HELL WAS HAPPENING? It was like Jack had forgotten that they were pretending. He didn't even really like her—did he? She drove him insane, so why was he suddenly acting so possessive? God, she hoped he wouldn't turn into an obsessed stalker. Cece would never let her hear the end of it.

"That's just semantics, is it not?" His eyes narrowed slightly.

"What?" he'd lost her.

"You're planning a hookup with the next guy while we're still actively hooking up. And there's no way I'm letting that happen."

Was he jealous? This whole arrangement had been his idea. What did he think would happen when their time was over?

"So because I'm pretending to be your fiancée, you think you can tell me what to do a week from now? When you're back to your life and I'm back to mine?" She hadn't meant to shout, but holy shit, this guy didn't own her just because they had spent a few days together.

He reeled back like she'd slapped him. She needed a minute

because this whole conversation was ridiculous. But Jack's eyes widened as he looked past her, and his shoulders dropped.

Oh no.

She turned, knowing what she would see before she did. Her stomach bottomed out at the sight of the Hill brothers wearing matching shocked expressions.

She glanced back at Jack; his jaw was locked and he wouldn't meet her gaze. Crap, how could she mess that up so badly? She took a shaky breath. Losing her cool and yelling at him had been an immature response to the situation. A tight fist latched around her heart, squeezing at the idea of ruining this for him.

Even if they weren't going to see each other after tomorrow, she didn't want to leave on a bad note. But how could she fix it?

"I'm—"

"Don't." Jack held up his hand to cut her off. He finally turned his attention to her, emotions warring in his eyes. She couldn't tell whether he was disappointed or pissed. The set of his jaw screamed pissed, but the shadows in his eyes looked more like hurt. "Go up to our room and let me deal with this."

Shoulders slumped, she grabbed the room key from him when he held it out to her. Once the elevator doors closed behind her, she leaned back against the wall and sighed.

The last thing she wanted was for Jack to suffer. Especially because of her. He'd been so good to her. She swallowed back her tears, hating that she'd failed him.

Her phone buzzed. Another fucking text. She had no intention of hooking up with Mike next week. Or ever. Being with Jack this week had made her realize some guys weren't total dipshits and she needed to develop standards. She'd been trying to find the words to tell Mike she wasn't interested when Jack freaked out.

It might have helped if she'd just told Jack she wasn't

hooking up with the guy anymore. Why was hindsight always so freaking accurate?

Shockingly, it wasn't Mike who'd texted.

Mom: Everything happens in perfect time. Be patient and trust the process while you work for what you want.

She couldn't stop the eye roll as she read her mom's inspirational message for the day.

Yeah. Okay, Mom. She wasn't sure how anything in her life would work out at the moment, but what she did know was that she couldn't stay here any longer. It was time to pack her stuff and go home. And when she got there, she needed to take a good hard look at her life and figure out what she really wanted.

21

JACK STARED at the elevator as the silver panels locked shut and the numbers above the door rose. Everything he'd been working for was on the line. He'd have to turn around and face the music. Face the Hill family and try to salvage things. But every part of his being screamed for him to follow Kelly. Because what happened with this account was far less concerning than the knowledge that his crazy girl thought they were going their own ways next week.

"Jack?" Ken prompted.

It was time. He sighed and spun around.

"I don't even know what to say." Jack shifted his weight on his feet and glanced over toward the elevator again when it opened, his heart squeezing when the woman stepping out wasn't Kelly. "I thought I needed to be something I wasn't to win you over. And I can't think straight with that woman spinning through my life like a tornado." He glanced at the elevator again, even though he knew Kelly wouldn't come back for him. "I'm sorry I lied."

Ken shook his head. "You didn't need to bring a fake fiancée to impress us, Jack. The way you carry yourself, your ideas, your dedication, they all speak for themselves. Not to mention your past work. We were thrilled when we heard you were coming instead of that coworker of yours."

Jack cocked a brow. "What?"

Walt, Ken's brother, nodded. "We've met Larry a few times, and we don't mesh. But we've heard good things about you. And you've spent this week proving them all true."

"Thanks." Until a few months ago, that probably wouldn't have surprised him. But the fiasco with his last account had fucked up everything he'd worked for.

Walt continued, but Jack couldn't resist peering over at the elevator again as the doors opened. He should be giving the Hills his attention, but he was dying to get upstairs and talk to Kelly. There was no way this hadn't become more than an arrangement to her.

"Jack." Ken cleared his throat, pulling his attention back to the matter at hand. "The way you watch the elevators every time the doors open tells me this isn't what needs your attention right now. Because the account isn't what matters."

He shook his head. "No, don't think that. It matters. More than anything."

Ken put a firm hand on his shoulder. "It matters. But not as much as her."

Jack tried to pull it together and focus on Ken and Walt. This contract mattered. His father's approval mattered.

"Don't." Walt shook his head.

"You don't need to explain." Ken smiled. "I love my business. I love my job. But when Linda needs me, I push my work aside. Probably more than is reasonable. Because there's important. And then there's *important*. Don't think we don't know the difference."

Jack tilted his head, digesting the man's words.

"We'll talk later," Walt assured him.

"Thanks." Jack forced a smile before jogging to the elevators. He needed to talk to Kelly. They could fix this. He was sure of it. And although Kelly was probably freaking out about spilling the beans of their fake relationship, it didn't seem to be an issue with his potential clients. With everything out in the open, maybe they could take time to explore this thing between them. They just needed to talk.

Jack knew they were on different pages, yet he was still floored when he walked into the room. Watching her fold her clothes and carefully pack them into her bag made his stomach bottom out.

She was going to leave without talking things through?

What the hell?

She glanced over her shoulder at him but didn't meet his eyes before turning her attention back to the clothes she was tucking into her bag. "I'm sorry. That was just the worst timing —like ever." Her shoulders slumped.

"I'm not worried about that." He glared at the bag, still baffled by how quickly she'd cleared out her things. "But we need to talk."

"Oh." She finally turned to him, then bit her lip and studied the contents of her suitcase. "Did you want the stuff you bought for me back? I didn't even think about leaving it."

"*Clothes? Are you fucking kidding me?*" Did she really think he gave two shits about any of her stuff?

She spun toward him, eyes going wide. "I said I was sorry. If I could, I'd go back and make sure I didn't say anything that could have been overheard. I get that you're mad. But what do you want me to do? Eventually we had to 'break up.'" She used air quotes on the last two words.

The ground crumbled beneath Jack's feet.

She really believed this was nothing more than an arrangement. He wasn't sure whether that was a punch to his gut or a knife to his heart. Either way, his chest was so tight he could barely breathe. He'd never gotten attached to a woman, even after months of sleeping together, and he'd never understood when they'd complain so dramatically about it. But the blank stare Kelly was giving him now made him want to throw up.

She was really walking away. He wanted to drop to his knees. Beg her to give him time to prove there was something real between them, but pride kept him on his feet.

He cleared his throat.

"Fine, let me write you a check."

The shirt in her hands snapped as she flung it. "*What*?" She hissed. "Are you for real right now?" Her mouth hung open and her eyes blazed with fury.

He paused, at a loss for words. His brain was screaming *abort*. He knew he'd massively mis-stepped, but he wasn't sure how. Kelly was a complex puzzle he desperately wanted to spend more time figuring out.

But she didn't want that. Right?

"You really still plan to *pay* me?" Her voice went up three octaves, and it was clear the answer should be no. But he wasn't sure why. "I get that I'm an idiot and messed up big time. But way to make me feel like a prostitute."

She shoved the last few things in her bag and snapped it shut.

What? Did that mean she thought there was something between them too? Before he could process exactly what she meant, she pushed past him and strode toward the door, letting it slam behind her.

Why did *he* suddenly feel like the asshole?

22

MONEY? Really? After everything, he was going to pay her? In the last few days, they had become so much more than a stupid paid arrangement. In her mind, they'd established something like a friendship. She wanted to help him, and she cared about him. She loved the way he laughed and called her crazy girl. The feel of his hand on her. The expression he made when he was working through the details of his presentation. And she thought he cared too, at least a little. Even the hand squeezes and hugs when they were alone seemed like more. And yet he wanted to *pay* her.

Her jaw clenched so tight it ached.

"Kelly. Stop for a minute." Janice's voice echoed through the lobby as she stepped through the glass doors that exited onto the street. Pausing on the sidewalk, she sighed. She liked Janice, and now Janice knew about the lie. But it was time to face the music.

"I heard what happened." Janice peered down at her bag. "Are you leaving?"

If she had heard, why did that fact surprise her?

Kelly swallowed hard as the woman gave her an assessing look.

"I messed everything up for Jack." She toed the sidewalk with the tip of her red wedge.

Janice chuckled. "Oh please, you didn't mess anything up but that man's heart."

Kelly froze. "What?"

"I don't know why it's taking my brothers so long to offer your man the account, but it's a sure thing. They loved what he put together, and they enjoy working with him. He checks all their boxes," Janice assured.

A weight lifted from Kelly's shoulders. The news was a relief, yet she still had this kernel of unhappiness deep in her stomach.

"But I wanted to talk to you about *you*," Janice went on.

"Me?" She tipped her head.

"I want to offer you a job," the older woman began. "No reason to stand their catching flies, Kelly."

She snapped her mouth closed. "A job?"

"My assistant decided not to return from maternity leave, and I've been using temps." Janice eyed the sky as she shook her head. "These people don't even have a basic understanding of chemistry, and when I've found someone who does, they can't handle social settings. I've been impressed with the way you've handled yourself in any situation."

Kelly couldn't stop the chuckle that escaped from her lips. "You mean how I pretended to be engaged to someone?"

"Oh, stop." Janice waved her off. "You two will work it out."

"There's nothing to work out. It was an arrangement." The word came out harsher then she meant, but her annoyance over how he'd tried to pay her was creeping back in.

"I see the way he looks at you." She patted Kelly's hand.

"He's smitten. And that man is the type who goes after what he wants." Janice winked.

She thought back to the look Jack had given her as she left the room.

"Right now, he's pissed."

"Yup." Janice chuckled. "Sounds like marriage to me. He'll go from smitten to being mad at you and then back to smitten. The cycle of love."

Love? She shook her head. "Even if you were right, he lives in LA."

Janice grinned. "If you took the job I'm offering and Jack accepts our contract, you two will be working together here."

Jack would be working here, in North Carolina? The idea shot through her like a roller coaster, the thrill before the drop.

He'd never mentioned staying in the state. Did he know?

If they worked together, she'd have to watch him move on. Date someone else. Acid swirled in her stomach at the idea.

"Can we get back to the job offer?" Janice asked.

Kelly nodded and listened as she laid out the job details. It was part executive assistant, part lab assistant. She'd be dumb to turn down such an amazing opportunity. But she just couldn't say yes. The kernel of discomfort grew.

Why didn't she want the job?

23

IT HAD BEEN two days since Kelly had slammed the door and left him reeling. And in that time, he'd been informed that he'd won the Hill account. He should be ecstatic. He'd taken his father's jet back to LA last night, but being home felt wrong, empty.

His apartment was too quiet, and he'd yet to feel like he wanted to pull his hair out. Even his eye had stopped twitching. He should be rejoicing in the lack of frustration, and yet a dark cloud hung over him.

He pushed through the revolving door into the main office of the Nickles Group. The meeting with his dad was scheduled to start in fifteen minutes. A week ago, walking into his father's office with the Hill account in his hand had been his life's goal. Now, although it was good news, he felt nothing but hollow.

Plus there was their stipulation that required the head of marketing to work on site. He hadn't been privy to that information until he was offered the contract. But had his dad known the whole time? His father had always expected Jack to take over the Nickles Group, and he couldn't do that from the mountains of North Carolina.

But Ken and Walt were adamant that Jack was the only account manager they wanted. Jack shook his head at the craziness of it all. He wanted to impress them so badly, and though he'd gone about it in the wrong way, they still wanted him.

"Dad," he said as he walked into his father's office. His father stood at the windows that overlooked downtown. He turned at Jack's voice. The tall blond man looked at least ten years younger than his fifty-six years.

"Jack." His father stepped around his desk, extending his hand. "Congratulations, son. I knew you could do it. The Hills are so thrilled to bring you on."

"Thanks, but I thought you wanted me to learn how to run the company so I could take over when you retire."

"Of course I do. But that starts by giving you accounts like this so you can get the hands-on experience." His dad smirked. "Besides, I have no plans to retire for at least another fifteen years. Who knows, maybe we can add another satellite location in that time."

"Satellite location?" Jack parroted.

"Yes," his father said, putting his hands in his pockets and smiling. "Take over your first big account and work at the Hills' corporate office like they want. They need someone focused and dedicated to get their marketing campaign for this vitamin water going. And they made it clear they want it to be you. After a year, we can get an office up in Charlotte." His dad raised a brow. "You get them up and running, then step back. It's how you grow the business. And this is the perfect way for you to learn."

Well, shit. How could he say no to that? His father was trusting him to run an account like this and oversee his own location. The gesture spoke volumes.

But when Ken had come to him with the marketing contract, he'd told Jack that Janice was hell bent on bringing

Kelly on staff too. And he wasn't sure he could see her every day and not want more.

The time apart hadn't done anything for Jack's feelings. In fact, it almost made them stronger. He missed her. Far more than he should. After all, they'd only known each other for a few days. Last night, he spent an hour watching her TikToks just to see her smile.

God, he was fucking pathetic. He should probably find out whether she'd taken the job Janice offered.

"Is there some other reason you're reluctant to accept this account?"

His father's forehead was creased with worry. The CEO of the Nickles group was gone, and in his place was Jack's dad.

"If there's a problem, you can talk to me."

Jack sighed. "Things didn't work out with Kelly..."

His father leaned forward. "I thought you said she might come out for a weekend. Did the fake fiancée thing blow up badly?"

The feeling of disappointment he'd grown accustomed to over the last several months hit him like a tidal wave.

"Yeah." Jack bowed his head, steeling himself for the lecture he was sure to get.

But instead, his dad chuckled. "I have no idea what possessed you to pretend you were engaged. Dan and I had a good laugh at your expense about the entire thing. I don't know the full story, so why don't you fill me in?"

Jack shook his head but dove into the details of the whole crazy week, starting from the moment he climbed into the back seat of Kelly's car.

His father shook his head with a deep sigh. "I've told your mom for years that you'd settle down once you met a woman who would keep you on your toes."

"She makes me insane, Dad. Like makes my eye twitch and

my head hurt insane, but I can't stay away from her." Jack rubbed his hand over his face and slumped into the chair.

"So she's like your mother, then?" Again, his father laughed. "I've always said that running this company is ten times easier than figuring out your mom. But love is like that. Half the time I feel like I'm guessing, the other half, I'm just giving her what she wants."

Jack swallowed and looked into his dad's green eyes. "You two have always made it look easy."

"It's definitely not easy, but it's worth it, and we're not quitters. Have you tried talking to Kelly since you left Asheville?" He leaned back, his leather chair creaking as he got comfortable.

Jack shook his head. What would he say? He wasn't even sure what happened. But he'd had a few days to stew on the events of the week, and he was sure that what he and Kelly had was real.

"You're heading back there, right?" his dad asked. "Go talk to her, tell her what you want."

But how could he chase someone who didn't want to be caught?

24

KELLY STARED, slack-jawed, digesting the details of the offer her boss had just made her. What the heck? For months, Kelly had floated aimlessly, having no idea what she was going to do with her life, and now, all of a sudden, people were flinging job offers at her left and right. She'd gone from no career prospects to two full-time job offers in a week.

"I thought you'd be happier." Ashley tucked a lock of blond hair behind her ear and tilted her head as Kelly tried to find the words she wanted to say.

"I-I am happy. I just—Can I think about it? I got another job offer this weekend, and I'm not sure what I should do."

"I was hoping to snatch you up to help me run the catering side of things at The Dock, but I can't say I'm surprised you're getting job offers. Who am I competing with?"

Kelly explained the situation she'd found herself in last week and the job offer from Janice as Ashley stared at her with wide eyes.

"Have you ever seen that movie...?" Ashley trailed off.

"*Pretty Woman*?" Kelly chuckled. "I know. It's like I lived it. Only I wasn't hired to be a hooker."

Jack would never have to pay a hooker. He probably had a line of women waiting for him when he got back to LA. The idea made her chest ache.

Ashley shook her head. "Only you, Kelly. These things could only happen to you. You should take the offer from Janice. You've been a huge asset to me for months, but chemistry is your passion, and if my boyfriend taught me anything these last six months, it's that we should all follow our passion."

"Yeah." Kelly should want this job. But would working with Jack be awkward? She desperately wanted to ask his opinion about the job, and she'd give just about anything to see him again, but she couldn't just text him out of the blue, right? Besides, what would she even say?

Hey, it feels weird not talking to you? That was dumb.

Ashley promised to give her time to think about the job. But as she pulled out of the parking lot of the catering office, her car headed toward her parents' house. Her mom might be guilty of texting the most ridiculous quotes, but her parents' advice never steered her wrong. Telling them she needed their help equated to eating crow, but she didn't know who else to go to. Still, the pep talk she gave herself in the driveway before she could climb out of the car took a solid five minutes.

When she stepped inside, they were sitting at the kitchen table with cups of coffee. Neither tried to hide their surprise at seeing her.

"I have a major problem and need your help." The words were out of her mouth before she even crossed the threshold into the kitchen.

Her dad's eye twitched, and her mom sighed before she asked, "How much money do you need?"

Kelly shook her hand. "It's not that. Ashley offered me a full-time position as an events manager at The Dock. It's here in town, and I love Ashley. And it could be good. But I got this *other* offer from the owner of Hill Water. I'm sure you've heard of them. They have the green label and make that new Water Plus, that vitamin water."

Her parents both stared at her with wide eyes.

"Anyway, she wants me to be her executive assistant slash lab assistant. And I'm not sure what to do. They're two very different jobs, and I know what to expect with Ashley, but the other opportunity is amazing and—"

"Slow down." Her mom stood in front of her now, cradling her face in her hands. "Are you saying your problem is that you have two good career opportunities?"

She nodded. "Yeah." She blew out a long breath. "I don't know what to do."

Her mom chuckled and released her face. "Honey, that's not a *problem*. That's a decision you have to make. Sit down and give us the details."

"How did you find this assistant job?" her father asked as he pushed out her chair with his foot.

A sense of calm washed over her as she flopped into the wooden chair that she'd spent hours in growing up. This was what she needed. She smiled as she jumped into her explanation.

"We're so proud of you," her mom said when she'd finished filling them in. "It sounds like the position with the Hills will give you the opportunity to follow your passion in science while still connecting with people, and it'll give you diversity so you don't feel tied to one thing."

"I don't know. I might have to move. I guess I could commute, but it's over an hour each way. And all that Ubering put a lot of miles on my poor car." Kelly slumped against the back of the chair.

Her mom waved off the statement. "We can help. Whatever you need."

Kelly stared at them with wide eyes. They'd cut her off months ago, and now they were willing to help her?

"We're here to support you, and we're proud of you," her dad said after a moment of silence. "We wanted you to settle down and figure out what you wanted to do with your life. When you quit nursing school so suddenly, we were concerned that jumping into things, then promptly quitting to try something new would become a pattern. You needed to find yourself. And it sounds like you've done that. Or at least you're heading in the right direction. But we can help you figure out the logistics regardless of which opportunity you choose."

She spent another hour talking through her choices and what changes each would require. By the time she headed home, she knew what she needed to do. But why did the thought of taking the job with Janice make her feel sick? She needed wine. Or ice cream.

At home, Cece was lounging on the sofa, absorbed in one of the scripted reality shows she loved. Kelly dashed over, plopped down at her best friend's feet, and blurted out, "I have to take the job at Hill Water, and I don't want to, but I don't know why."

"So we finally need the wine?" Cece chuckled, tossing her hands into the air. "It's about time we got here."

Kelly followed Cece to the island that separated the living room from the kitchen. "I don't know what my issue is."

"I do." Cece scoffed. "You have *feelings* for Jack. Remember that getting attached conversation where you talked about TikTok, and I tried to deep dive into your feelings?"

Kelly rolled her eyes. "I've told you already. It was just pretend."

Cece narrowed her eyes. "If that were the case, then why didn't you take the money?"

Kelly opened her mouth, but no words came out. She wished she hadn't told Cece how upset she was when Jack tried to pay her.

"How do you live this far down the river of denial? Maybe

after a few drinks, you'll be more willing to admit it to yourself."

Cece grabbed a bottle from the wine rack that sat on top of the refrigerator and dug through a drawer for a corkscrew. Kelly turned to the cabinet and grabbed two glasses before following her into the living room.

"Maybe I could work for your dad." Kelly chuckled. "Seriously, the man candy in that fire house would keep me happy." Although none of them were as handsome as Jack. Something about his blond hair and smirk worked perfectly. She missed the way his green eyes turned dark when he looked at her. And the way his eye twitched when she was making him crazy. She just missed *him*.

Cece snickered, shaking her head. "Yeah, that's a hard no. My father would lose his shit if he was stuck with you for more than an hour." Cece poured a few inches of crimson liquid into each glass. "Let's be real."

"Real how?"

"If there's nothing between you and Jack, then how about I date him? You yourself said he's the type of guy anyone would pick for their friend." She didn't break eye contact as she lifted her glass and took a slow sip.

Kelly loved Cece. And sure, she wanted a good guy for her. But that didn't mean she wanted to share Jack.

Her mind raced.

The way his hand felt on the small of her back.

The press of his lips against hers.

His smile.

The way he lifted her and cradled her against him.

The sound of his voice when he called her crazy girl.

Their conversations.

His intensity.

She didn't want to share any of it.

"Cece." Kelly swallowed hard. "I really like him."

"Finally." Her best friend flopped back against the sofa. "Welcome to reality. Thanks for joining the rest of us. Now call Janice, accept the job, and then text Jack and ask to talk. Tell him you want to try something real."

"What if he doesn't want that?" Just the idea made her stomach sink with dread. "I might have messed everything up."

Cece narrowed her eyes. "Just talk to him. You'll never know if you don't try."

She took a long sip of her wine and thought about Cece's words. What was she supposed to do?

25

JACK PICKED up his phone for the hundredth time since he'd touched down in North Carolina. His fingers hovered over *Crazy Girl*, but he locked the screen and set the device back on the desk. He still didn't know what to say. It was the most important pitch of his life, and he was at a loss.

His dad's advice about winging it or giving her what she wanted was impossible because Jack had no idea *what* the woman wanted. He needed to talk to her. He knew that. But he wanted to do it in person. Look into her eyes and tell her how he felt.

But he needed the right words.

Maybe he should suggest they meet up for dinner or coffee or something. If he could remember how to get to her apartment, he'd show up at the door in a heartbeat. But then again, maybe he'd have the same issue he had every fucking time he picked up the phone.

Because if she said no—to dinner or coffee or even to feeling anything, to trying again for real—it was over. And the possibility froze him solid.

A knock on the doorframe brought him back to the

present. He was settling into things at the corporate office of Hill Water, but he was still getting used to the number of people who kept popping in. Most stopped by to introduce themselves, but the constant stream hadn't stopped even after two days.

He looked up at the open doorway, and his eyes widened. All dark hair and curves. He took in her black leggings, letting his gaze run over her hip and up to her shoulder, where the gray sweater hung loosely. Collarbones and creamy skin. He swallowed hard before finally meeting her bright blue eyes. Jesus, she was beautiful, and it floored him every time he looked at her.

His heart sped up.

"Hey." Kelly's pouty lips turned up slightly.

"Hi," he croaked and cleared his throat.

She crossed her arms, pushing her breasts up and making his mouth go dry. His brain screamed at him to invite her in and tell her to sit down. But his heart pounded in his ears and his words caught in his throat as he took in every inch of her skin, the waves in her hair, each curve of her body. He longed to touch her. Feel her against him. To hear her laugh, moan.

"Congrats on..." She waved her hand around the office.

He didn't give a shit about the job at the moment, but he nodded. "Thanks." He took a breath, racking his brain for the right words. Because this—she—mattered too much to mess it up. "Come in?"

Hesitantly, she scanned the space and swallowed before moving the five feet from his door to stand behind the chair across the desk. Her hand rested on the leather back, her dark blue polish catching his attention as she gripped the seat back.

He tried not to be discouraged when she didn't sit. But dread grew in the pit of his stomach when she wouldn't meet his eye either.

"I don't know if you heard, but, um," she tucked a long

wave behind her ear and cleared her throat, "I start here, as Janice's assistant, tomorrow."

The words turned up at the end. Like she was hoping for something. But it wasn't news to him. There was no doubt in his mind that she would rock her new position.

"And since this is clearly..." She shrugged and waved her hand between them. "I didn't want to do this on my first day."

He shook his head and swallowed hard. His chest caved in on itself as the realization hit. She'd come to clear the air. But this was his chance to finally talk to her. To tell her how he felt. To take a chance without letting his pride stop him.

"I came by to make sure we were...that it wouldn't be a problem, you know. Us j-just," a small crease appeared between her eyes as her brow furrowed, "working together."

The words echoed in his ears. *Just* working together.

If that was what she wanted, he'd respect her wishes, but damn, seeing her here every day would crush him. Even the idea of putting her in the coworker only category felt wrong. Not being able to touch her. To whisper in her ear, to make her moan his name. But he'd do it.

"It won't," he assured with a fake smile that every fiber of his being wanted to rebel against. "I'll be the best damn coworker ever. I know this job is important to you."

This opportunity for her in the lab was huge. He wanted it for her.

Finally, her blue eyes met his, almost like they were pleading, but for what, he didn't know. He'd given her everything, and she didn't want it.

"Right." She shrugged. "S-see you tomorrow."

She turned, but he swore he saw tears in her eyes before she looked away. But she walked out of his office without looking back.

That was it. Over. She'd walked away again. Just like when the door clicked shut behind her at the hotel, he wanted to chase her. More than anything. But just like last time, he didn't have the right words.

He sank into his chair and dropped his head into his hands. What could he have said differently? He scoffed. *Anything*.

His heart skipped.

Who the fuck cared if he had the *perfect* words? He just needed to try *some* words.

26

SHE SHUT Jack's door behind her and swallowed hard. That fake as hell smile and the assurance that work was important. That said it all.

She was thankful she'd gotten this out of the way before she started her new job, because after that, there was no way she would have made it through her first day if she'd waited until then. Today she could go home, cry, and put it all behind her. And tomorrow, she could smile like Jack did and pretend it was fine.

The lump that had taken up residence in her throat grew, and her eyes burned. Maybe it wasn't too late. Maybe Jack never thought of it as anything more than an agreement. Thankfully, her new position would keep her on the other side of the building in the R&D area.

She weaved through the hall and into the lobby of Hill Water.

"Kelly!" Ken's voice echoed through the open space.

She twirled, searching for him, finally spotting him on the open staircase leading to the second floor. It was lunchtime, and the lobby was full of people coming and going and milling about. Every time she came in, employees were chatting. The environment the Hills had created was the friendliest she'd ever seen. That meant there was no escaping without at least a hello.

She forced a smile and a small wave.

"I thought you started tomorrow," Ken said as he and Walt descended the steps.

"I do, but—"

"*Kelly*!" Jack's voice rang out behind her, and she spun again. He was practically running down the hallway toward her. "Wait."

"What's the matter?"

He pulled to an abrupt stop in front of her and yanked at his tie. "I came to the hills of North Carolina because I thought the only way to sublimate in Nickles Group was to acquire the Hill account. I thought it was essential." He shook his head. "But the truth is, I was at a pivotal moment where I had to master the contrast between important and vital." He searched her face desperately, his brow furrowed.

All she could do was scan their surroundings, noting all the eyes on them. She didn't even know the definition of some of those words, let alone how to respond.

"I—" She wet her lips. "English, Jack," she mumbled.

He shut his eyes and took a deep breath.

"I always thought Jack from that nursery rhyme you like was an asshole." He tossed his hands in the air. Although that made even *less* sense, she had to chuckle, because at least she could understand him.

"Let me finish." He took three more steps so he stood toe to toe with her. "What kind of guy drags the woman he cares about down with him when he falls?"

A few people around them laughed, but all Jack did was watch her.

"The thing is, when you're standing next to the most *beautiful, intelligent* woman," he murmured, his green eyes burning

135

into her with an intensity that flipped her stomach, and closed the small gap between them. "A woman who makes you laugh and supports you and *fits* you better than anyone ever has," keeping her pinned with his gaze, he lifted his hand, his warm palm cupping her cheek, "and you realize you're tumbling head over heels, you've got to reach out and bring her with you." He swallowed, and she felt his shiver as she rested her hand on his chest. "Because she needs to be next to you, because she's not just important to you; she's *vital* to your existence."

She blinked hard at the tears in her eyes. She understood that perfectly. When her tongue darted out to run along her bottom lip, his attention locked there, and he leaned in slowly, giving her plenty of time to pull away. But no part of her wanted to.

His lips met hers softly, not heated with their normal fire. No, this was a gentle promise.

Jack pulled back, resting his forehead against hers. "Can we try again?" His hot breath brushed across her lips with each word.

"For real this time?" she asked.

"Like sups real. Literally."

She pinched his side. "We don't even speak the same language."

"I'll buy you a dictionary." He bit back a laugh as her eyes narrowed. But the smile fell from his face quickly, replaced with an intensity she'd come to love about him. "Honestly, I *love* that about you. You remind me not to take everything so seriously. To be in the moment. I need that. I need you."

"You realize I'm going to make you crazy, right?"

"I'm counting on it."

27

CATCHING up with her best friend over dinner was exactly what Kelly needed. She'd loved living with Jack for the last month, but it meant she didn't see Cece as much as she'd like.

The humid August air blew in her windows as she drove toward home, chuckling over the drama Cece had found herself in. Her bestie needed to figure things out, because the planner that she was, she wouldn't survive very long without one. Especially because her dad would lose his shit when he found out about his daughter and his newest crew member.

Though her own parents had welcomed Jack easily, even though he was older, so maybe she was wrong. She snorted. No way was she wrong.

She tapped the wheel anxiously. The last five months had been perfect, but Jack had been in California for a week, and she couldn't wait to get home and see him.

An ear-piercing ping blasted through the speakers, jarring her. Crap, she wasn't sure she'd ever get used to the Bluetooth setup in her new car. It made her jump every time.

She smiled as the car's automated voice read the text message out loud.

Jack said: Just got in. Are you on your way home yet? Don't forget to stop for gas.

She had to chuckle every time he reminded her. Once she pulled into the driveway, she got out and dialed Jack.

"Please don't tell me you ran out of gas again."

"Well..." she started, holding back her laugh.

"Are you freaking kidding me? There's no reason to get gas in small doses anymore. You can use the credit card I gave you. I *want* you to." He blew out a long breath. "Where are you? Grabbing my keys and the gas can. Thank God I refilled it. Just tell me the road has a good shoulder."

She opened the front door and stepped in as he came around the corner from the kitchen in jeans and a white T-shirt. One look at her had his eye twitching.

"Good news. I didn't run out of gas."

He shook his head and chuckled.

"But..."

His eyes narrowed. "You didn't stop, did you?"

"Sorry, not sorry." She shook her head as she walked toward him. "I was in a rush to get home."

"Really?" he said, a smirk playing on his lips. "Why was that?"

"It's been a week." Kelly wrapped her arms around his waist and tilted her head back to look up at him. "I missed you."

The house they shared had felt extra big and lonely over the last few days.

"I missed you too." Jack ran his nose along her jaw and nipped at her ear. "But we're taking your car to work tomorrow so I can make sure you have a full tank of gas."

"You're the best."

He grabbed her by the ass and lifted her, and she wrapped her legs around his waist as he carried her to the stairs.

"Would you be mad if I was pregnant?"

She jostled a bit as Jack missed a step, but he caught them before they tumbled down the stairs. He cleared his throat, standing three steps from the top. "No."

It was great how certain that was.

"That's what I thought." She smiled, but the man remained frozen in place. She glanced around. "Are we not going up?"

He scaled the last few stairs and then set her on the bed.

"Kel," he said, hovering over her. "I'm not mad, but is there something you need to *tell* me?" His green-eyed gaze was intense as his breath danced across her face.

She shook her head. "Absolutely not. I didn't bury the lede." She quoted that because that was Jack's thing. Start with the important stuff. "We have *no* gas."

His eye twitched. "Okay...but are you pregnant?"

"What? *No.*" Kelly's eyes widened. "Not *me.* Why would you think that?" She was on birth control. Although that was kinda tonight's theme. It didn't always work.

Jack smiled and took a deep breath. "With you, my life will never be boring, crazy girl."

EPILOGUE

JACK PROPPED himself against the wooden doorframe that led into the bedroom and studied his beautiful wife. A year and a half ago, he was convincing her to pretend to be his fiancée, and now they were honeymooning in Bora Bora. The destination was the easiest part of the wedding.

Weddings were *a lot.* And his parents had so many requests. Thankfully, Kelly was as laid back about the planning as she was with everything else. He loved her more every day.

She stood in the center of the bedroom, looking down through the glass floor in awe. "I can *literally* see fish."

Might be the first time she'd used the word correctly.

"You want to swim with them, or you want to eat first?" He crossed one foot over the other and took a sip of his beer.

"I want to eat. I'm, like, literally starving."

And they were back to literally meaning *ridiculously very.*

He chuckled as he moved into the room. She turned to gaze out at the ocean, and he put his arms around her, his chest pressing against her back. The doors that led from the bedroom to the large deck were open, and the expansive turquoise water was all they could see for miles.

"This is even more amazing in person," she whispered.

"It is." He smiled. Even though the location was amazing, the woman in his arms was what it made it perfect. "But a week alone with my gorgeous wife *anywhere* is my dream."

Between planning the wedding and their careers, the last six months had been hectic for both of them. Kelly had been promoted to Research and Development Lab Manager at Hill water, while Jack trained his replacement since he was now running the Nickles Group's Asheville office.

At first, his father had scoffed at the idea of opening an office in Bumblefuck Asheville instead of Charlotte or Nashville. He grinned at the memory of the look on the man's face. But Jack's whole world was in Bumblefuck, so there was nowhere else he'd be. *That* his dad understood.

"Come on, crazy girl. Let's grab something to eat and check out the resort." He skimmed over her hips with his fingertips, pressing her back against him. But Kelly pushed away and took off ahead of him. Always charging into the next adventure. He loved that about her, and he still couldn't believe he was the lucky guy who got to follow her into every tomorrow.

A NOTE FROM THE AUTHORS

Dear Reader (Jenni here),

When I dropped a pen name into *More than a Hero* for my character Morgan, AJ knew we needed to bring Kacie West's stories to life. Convincing me to do it with her was the easy part because I'm always willing to change directions and focus on something new. Anyone else have attention spam problems, or is it just me?

Kacie's debut novel came from the fact that we wanted to write our favorite tropes first. I thought we meant grumpy/sunshine, all the while, AJ was thinking we were doing snowed in. Then in the middle of the night, I came up with the crazy idea that we could make it Goldilocks, and I texted this to AJ. She, of course, thought I meant going a whole new way. But once I explained (in the morning at a reasonable hour), she loved the idea. And Goldilocks and the Grumpy Bear was born. Which then paved the way to our theme of funny smutty versions of popular nursery rhymes. If you've read *More than a Hero*, then you know Morgan was working on an Uber driver story, so we knew we just had to do that story.

Merging how we write, though, was a lot harder. AJ likes to

plan and know where the story is going straight from the start, and I like live with my characters for a while and get a feel of them. (AJ rolls her eyes about this.) But we're learning.—things like if AJ gets too far ahead of the bones of a book, I might come in, feel boxed into a corner, delete two chapters, and go a different way. Let's just say AJ understood where Jack was coming from a lot in this book, where as I was much more of a Kelly girl.

So now that Goldilocks got snowed in with the Grumpy Bear, and Jack brought Jill up the hill with him before Tumbling Head Over Heels together, what are we doing next? A spider starts a lot of problems for Little Miss Muffet and her hero, who will both be thrown completely off course by the eight-legged creature. Then, this fall, we'll pumpkin out the year with Peter, Peter, Pumpkin Eater. And we would love to have you join us for the entire trip.

Happy reading.

ALSO BY KACIE WEST

Goldilocks and the Grumpy Bear

ALSO BY JENNI BARA

More Than The Game

More Than Fine

More Than A Hero

More Than A Story

More Than Myself

Wishing for More

ALSO BY AJ RANNEY

Always Yours

Impossibly Yours

Wishing to be Yours

Want to see more of Half Moon Lake?

Check out Jackson and Ashley's story, a small-town enemies-to-lovers romance, and find out what happens when she's forced to work with her brothers best friend.

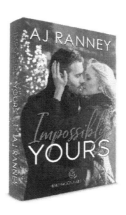

JACKSON

"Another." I rubbed the back of my neck and took in the room full of stupidly happy people, sliding the low-ball glass toward the bartender.

He arched a brow. "Shouldn't you be celebrating the lovely couple, not drowning your sorrows at the bar by yourself?"

"It's been a shit week, man. Just give me another one." I pinched my eyes closed in hopes of clearing my head. Then I downed another drink and pushed away from the bar.

I scanned the linen-covered tables. According to Bella and Ashley, the tablecloths were ivory, not white. They looked white to me, but I wasn't about to argue with the bride or her maid of honor.

A warm gust blew in from the lake, and I inhaled the mossy air that was infused with just a hint of pine. The glow from the lights lining the edge of the tent stood out against the dark sky. North Carolina's constant summer rain forced the just-in-case tent, but it had turned out to be a beautiful September night.

I loosened the bow tie that had me in a death grip. The damn things always choked me. I fucking hated monkey suits. This was my best friend's wedding, though, so I wouldn't complain, but I would have preferred something a lot less formal. A pair of well-worn pants and a dress shirt with the sleeves rolled was usually as fancy as I got. But as the best man, I did as I was told and wore the damn tux.

We hadn't always been close. Rhett Williams had been the quarterback of the high school football team when my family relocated from New York when I was sixteen. If we hadn't been paired as lab partners and connected over our shared interest in playing guitar, we probably wouldn't have become friends. And although we'd been tight for years, I couldn't help but wonder if he would've asked me to be his best man if his older brother Kyle wasn't currently deployed overseas.

My steps echoed against the floor as I made my way toward my mother. She winced, trying to push herself up from the chair she had settled into only five minutes ago. She'd spent too much time on her feet between the ceremony and the reception, and it was taking its toll.

"What the fuck is she doing?" I muttered. She needed to take it easy, *not* overdo it. She had pushed herself too hard all summer, which meant I'd had to cancel an important business trip scheduled for next week so I could be here to help her. Her surgery to repair the herniated disc wasn't *originally* planned until after the holidays, and even though my father, my sister, and I had offered to help her all summer, she was too proud to let us. Now she had no choice.

"Why don't you and Dad go home?" I grabbed her elbow to support her as she stood. Pain radiated through her tight smile. Her back had been a constant issue over the last year, and she couldn't stand the pain medication. In her mind, the loss of control she experienced when she took them far outweighed the pain-free hours.

Ridiculous.

"I can't leave yet. Rhett and Bella are still here. And I need to help Ashley make sure everything gets broken down and packed up in the van. If it's not done right, it'll be a mess to sort." She took half a step around me but hissed as her back gave out.

"Mom. *Sit down*," I urged, clutching her elbow again and trying to stay calm.

For the first time, I noticed the strands of gray hair and wrinkles that lined her forehead and breathed a sigh of relief at the surrender written all over her face.

My mother was one of the most stubborn people I knew. Well, maybe aside from her apprentice, Ashley. I swear the two of them wore me out—I was trying to get one to let me do what she'd asked of me and the other to accept the help I'd been asked to give.

It was probably time to let the catering business go, and even though I'd told my mom that twice now, she wasn't ready. She had started it because she enjoyed cooking, creating the menus, and planning events, but if she couldn't do much of that anymore, what was the point of keeping it? It wasn't even lucrative.

"Look, I got this. I'll help Ashley tonight." I'd already told her this earlier. "Go home and get off your feet." They'd moved her surgery up and wanted her to take it easy for the next two weeks.

Over my mom's shoulder, I locked eyes with my dad, who was heading toward us. He nodded as understanding passed between us. When he muttered something in Spanish, I knew he must have witnessed the same thing I had. Unless we were in Texas visiting his side of the family, he rarely pulled out his native tongue. And when he did, it was because he was frustrated.

"Time to go, Barbara." My dad's no-nonsense tone and my mom's sigh confirmed things. They were finally leaving.

"I'll find Ashley and see where she needs help." I bent down and placed a brief kiss on her cheek before turning to walk away.

"Make sure you load the van correctly!" she called after me.

"Yes, Mother." Because, of course, I never did anything right. I was the eternal bachelor who didn't truly have his shit together at thirty, according to my parents. In their minds, my success was merely a fluke rather than hard earned. My jet-setting lifestyle and casual relationships only enforced the irresponsible and unreliable image of me they'd created.

What most people didn't understand? I wasn't willing to settle. I worked hard for my success, no matter what others thought. And *I* was proud of it. But over the last year, I'd slowly gotten sick of the meaningless relationships. For a few years after some bad experiences, casual was what I wanted, but now? I was ready for more. Finding it had been the problem. The women I'd met were of two types. Each one either had a great personality, but we lacked chemistry, or the sex was great, but I couldn't stand to be in the same room with the chick while fully clothed.

I'd heard the rumors, knew what everyone thought. I'd been labeled the town's rich playboy. Letting people think what they wanted was easier than constantly trying to prove them wrong.

It didn't help that my parents were well off. People that didn't know me assumed that my money was handed to me. They saw the tattoos, my financial status, the lack of a regular nine-to-five, and a revolving door of women and made assumptions.

Just like the situation with Sophia. A child I desperately wanted to help but could only do so much for. And as hard as I fought, it was never enough. I failed. I failed *her*. Would the outcome have been the same if I were a woman?

Probably not. Because let's face it, I didn't fit the image the courts expected to see of a *responsible adult.*

I balled my hands into fists as I replayed the meeting I'd had with my lawyer.

But no, I couldn't go there. Not now. Not yet.

Lost in my thoughts, I rounded the corner of The Dock, the Williams family's restaurant, inn, and marina. I didn't see Ashley until it was too late, and I collided with her, sending the trays she'd had balanced in her arms crashing to the ground. At least I'd grabbed her arm to steady her on her heels before she toppled over with them.

"God dammit, Jackson. What the hell is wrong with you?" The fire in her azure eyes seared my skin as she glared at me. Though the fury didn't detract from the perfect way she filled out the dress that matched the color of her eyes and the vest I wore over my white tuxedo shirt.

"Sorry, I wasn't paying attention."

"Why am I not surprised? Do you *ever* consider *anyone* but yourself?" She yanked out of my hold and bent to pick up the trays. Her pinned-up blond hair bounced slightly, threatening to topple free.

Do not lose your cool. Do not lose your cool.

"Said I was sorry. Here, let me." I scooped the trays up and headed toward the van but paused mid-step and turned to face her. "You know, there're employees here to load this stuff up. Shouldn't you be enjoying the rest of your *brother's* wedding?"

She clenched her jaw and crossed her arms. "Your mother likes the van loaded a certain way. I'm just making sure it's done right."

How these two worked together, I had no clue. They were both stubborn in their own ways.

"Who's going to unload it tomorrow? It won't be my mom; I can guarantee that. She overdid it tonight."

"And it sure as hell won't be you. Like you'd bother to get up early on a Sunday to help me."

"Because you know me so well?" I gripped the trays tighter, my biceps and forearm muscles tightening, but let out a deep breath, hoping once more to reason with the woman who seemed intent on driving me to drink. "Look, let's enjoy the rest of the wedding. Miguel and Kelly will load up the van. I'll be there tomorrow at eight to help you unload it. Promise."

"Why am I not surprised you would want to pass the work off on other people?"

"We *pay* them! It's their job! Jesus Christ."

My attention landed on Kelly, our head server, as she made her way toward us.

"Let me take those." Kelly gestured to the trays I was still clutching. "You guys should go back out there. They're looking for you two. Something about a final dance with the whole wedding party." She nodded in the direction she had come from, then moved toward the van.

"You and Miguel know how to load the van the way my mom likes it, correct?" I asked.

Kelly's tight smile was answer enough. "Of course. That's one of the first things Mrs. Vargas and Miss Williams trained us to do."

"I've told you to call me Ashley," she huffed.

"Thank you, Kelly." I gripped Ashley by the elbow and turned her back toward the white tent. "Come on. Put your fake smile on and pretend you don't hate me while we dance."

"I'm not *that* good an actress," she sneered.

Even though I tried to stop it, the corner of my mouth twitched. "Well, for the sake of our best friends, I'm sure you can fake enjoying a five-minute dance with me."

"I bet you're very familiar with women faking with you."

I couldn't help it this time. I threw my head back and laughed. This girl had balls. Never one to back down and always determined to get in the last word. It was one of the reasons I'd spent the better part of the last fourteen years riling her up; I knew she'd throw it right back at me.

I shook my head. "Nope, their screams are always a hundred percent pure satisfaction. The only faking I've experienced has to do with personalities. They turn on the charm when they think I can give them the lifestyle they want. It's why I make it clear that all they'll get from me are mind-blowing orgasms and nothing more."

And with that, she was finally speechless.

Fuckin' A.

ACKNOWLEDGMENTS

Thank you to our wonderful readers, whose love for our characters sometimes even outweighs our own. Your love for the Metros men, the Evans family, and all the characters from Half Moon Lake is amazing. To our street and ARC teams, a big thank you for all your sharing, your reviews, your support, your shout-outs. You are all the best!

Thank you to our families for all your support and love. We couldn't do this without you! A special thank you to Ashley and Will for dealing with our constant phone calls to plot or tweak the things that aren't working. We know we annoy you both.

Beth, thank you for being so flexible and understanding with this book and everything. We are so glad we found you, and we will never stop singing your praises from the rooftop. You are amazing with your edits and proofreads and checking everything twice! You are thoughtful and detailed and amazing at keeping an author's voice. More than that, you are a friend who Jenni is so grateful to have in her life. Thank you for being the wonderful person you are.

Katie, thank you for all your endless help and support. You've been with Jenni since the start and added AJ along the way. We both love all your edits, comments, and suggestions. Without you, our stories would never be what they are.

Haley, thank you so much for all your help. Words can't

express how grateful we are for what you do. Jenni's constant "wait, I have a new plan/idea" that makes you pivot never fazes you, and AJ's schedules and need for a plan you make work too. We couldn't be more different and yet equally frustrating, and you take it all in stride.

Erica, thank you for all you do. You are the blurb master and the graphics queen. We never stop learning from you. Jenni can't express how thankful she is for all you do to teach and support her.

Daphne and Britt, thank you for being friends and teachers. The amount of knowledge and insight you have given is something that we are eternally grateful for. And your friendship is something we don't want to do without. Even the funny parts like Britt reading Jenni's thoughts. You two are the best. Everyone should check out the Havenport Series by Daphne Elliot and the Bristol Bay series by Brittanee Nicole because these two women have too much talent to not be known to every reader.

Annie, thank you for your cover help. You are never fazed by all the SOS help or the fact that half a world away, you are teaching wraps. And on top of that, you never hesitate to make time for a beta read. You rock! And everyone should check out The Temptation Series by Annie Charms.

And thank you, Amy Jo, for not only beta reading, but for all the beautiful book minis, bookmarks, and other swag you've made for us.

To all our author friends and beta readers, thank you for being supportive and inspiring writers. Kristin Lee, Alexandra Hale, Swati MH, Amanda Zook, Bonnie Poirier, JL Reed, Garry Michaels, Kat Long, Jane Poller, Lizzie Stanley, Blye Donovan, Raleigh Damson, Bethany Monaco Smith, Elyse Kelly, and so many, many more.

Jeff, thank you for being the final nit-picky check to make

sure everything is perfect. Becoming a romance reader wasn't on your to-do list, but Jenni's grateful you did it anyway!

To all our friends and family, a big thank you because we love you, and your support is something we are eternally thankful to have.

ABOUT THE AUTHORS

AJ fell in love with Morgan's pen name, Kacie West, from *More than a Hero* and talked Jenni into bringing her books to life. Kacie West was born as a real-life author, and the two began co-writing. AJ is the plotter, organizer, and planner, so she writes all the bones of the story, then sends it back to Jenni. Then, when AJ is busy with her two kids, husband, and her house full of animals, Jenni goes through to add, edit, and tweak it. Which sometimes includes line editing her own sentences more than a few times to make it all just right. Then while AJ works on more bones, Jenni goes back to her four kids and day job as a paralegal in family law, writing real life unhappily ever afters all day. AJ and Jenni have not only become co-authors but great friends, and they can't wait to bring more of Kacie West's stories to life.

Made in the USA
Middletown, DE
03 March 2023